The Jesus Diary

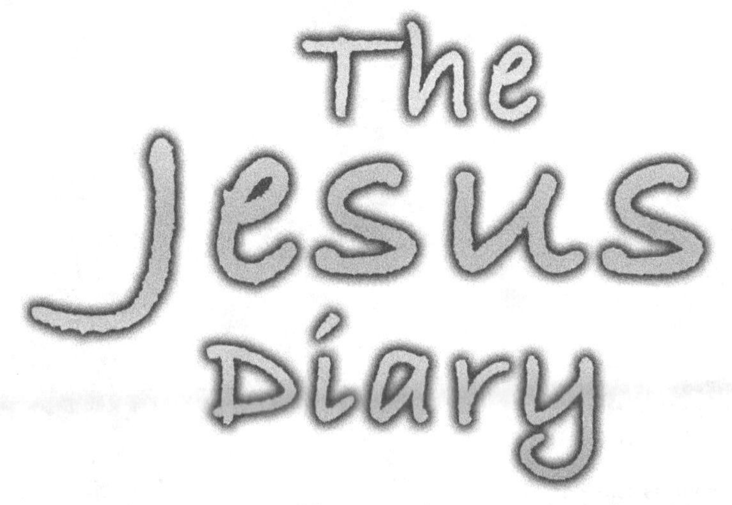

An Anonymous Observer's Record of the Life and Accomplishments of Our Savior

Dave Mishur

XULON PRESS

Xulon Press
2301 Lucien Way #415
Maitland, FL 32751
407.339.4217
www.xulonpress.com

Paperback ISBN-13: 978-1-6628-1350-4
Dust Jacket ISBN-13: 978-1-6628-1351-1
eBook ISBN-13: 978-1-6628-1352-8

In Memory of
Patricia Ann (Pochron) Mishur
The Saint I Married

Table of Contents

Prologue: Why this Book?

TO BE PRECISE, there are two questions: Why *This* Book, and why this book at *this* time? The first is easy to answer. The evangelists tell the story of our Savior in a fast-paced, almost telegraphic, style. Their goal was to record as much information about Jesus as possible as quickly and briefly as possible. The four Gospels, as a result, present an incredible amount of information in a highly condensed format.

The evangelists did not take notes. The Gospels are based on their individual recollections of what Jesus did, and when and where and to whom he did it. Thus there are significant differences in their stories. No one evangelist tells the whole story, and the creative mind is invited to embellish and expand it.

Thus this book: my attempt to humanize Jesus as he interacted with the world of his time. We believe that Jesus was true God and true man, like us in all ways except sin. He had real emotions, real feelings, and felt real joy and pain. In addition, the world around him offered a unique cast of characters: the Pharisees and other leaders of the people, as well as those with genuine problems: the lepers, the blind and lame; but most of all the sinners, whose repentance and faith he sought more than anything else.

Jesus interacted with them by healing their ills and their souls, but the Gospels say little of the reactions of those he cured. I try to show some of their emotion and joy, and also show the human side of Jesus without trivializing his deity.

The second question: Why this book at this time?

Despite our advancements in science, technology and medicine, humanity today remains just as flawed as at the time of Christ. We still have our Scribes and Pharisees.

This book includes certain instances of phoniness and pharisaical hypocrisy from the time of Christ. I was inspired by examples of the same sort of behavior in our world today. Readers are encouraged to make their own associations between the events and personalities of our day and those you read about in these pages.

So, this book is not really about the world of Jesus; it's about our world of today, which is adrift and in peril, ailing and in need of a good dose of Jesus.

While certain real people and events are chronicled here, this is completely and entirely a work of fiction. No aspersions, complaints or criticisms of anyone living or dead are intended. Any mistakes or errors of whatever kind are wholly my own. Readers are cautioned that the author of this fictitious diary could not possibly have known that Jesus was God, and so he may not always seem to accord him the devotional respect that we do today. Nor did he see the apostles as saints. To him, they were ordinary men, full of human faults and failings.

For the sake of authenticity, we have followed his text as closely as possible, including his stream-of-consciousness style, capitalization, and occasionally unorthodox sentence structure. It is, after all, just a diary.

If this book encourages even one reader to spend time with the Sacred Scriptures it will have been well worth the effort.

Introduction: How This Book Came to Be

IT WAS IN the 1970s, while on vacation, when we wandered into an antique store in central Illinois where we purchased what we thought was just an old ceramic water jug. The owner of the shop knew nothing of its provenance, as it was part of the inventory that came with the store when he bought it several years before.

It was an interesting jug, with a tight plug at the top. We couldn't remove it and, as there was no rattle or sound when we shook it, we assumed the jug was empty. It served as an interesting conversation piece in our home for many years. Our cat however, a polydactyl that would occasionally run around crazily, dislodged it from its shelf one night. I heard the crash and got up to inspect.

What I found was our old water jug lying in several pieces on the floor, and beside it, a tightly wound scroll. It had been inside the jar all along. I unrolled it carefully, saw that it was written in Latin, and carefully wrapped it up again for further examination in the morning. I took shots of it with my smartphone, as I knew old documents often degrade rapidly when exposed to the air. This translation is taken from those photos. It proved to be quite a remarkable document, and I am glad to share its contents with you.

About the author of the scroll we know nothing: Not even his name; but we know what he did. He kept a diary. He called it his Jesus Diary.

Having been on the scene at Bethlehem, he dedicated his life to follow and learn all he could about the child who was born there.

He followed him, step by step, year by year, diligently recording what he saw and heard and felt. His alert eyes and ears bring you face to face with Jesus.

This anonymous author provides first-hand testimony of many of the miracles and events in the life of Jesus, with vivid portrayals of the Savior, the people who loved him and followed him, and those who hated him enough to put him to death. This is his heart-felt narration of the activities and accomplishments of Jesus, the man who called himself the Son of God.

Although I am by no means a Latin scholar, I was able to render this translation of that ancient diary, hidden for centuries in a ceramic jug. I humbly present it to you hoping it will bring new meaning to the life of Jesus, and possibly to your own as well.

It's a Miserable Night in the City

> And so the people went, each one to his own city. Joseph went up from Nazareth in Galilee to Judea to the city of David called Bethlehem, because he was from the house and family of David. Luke 2.3

...ALL THESE PEOPLE milling about, pushing, shoving, jostling. Can't get anywhere. That's what happens when Caesar says he wants all the world to be counted. What Caesar wants, Caesar gets. And what you get is this insane mob. Oh, to be back home, with friends and a cup of wine, instead of here in this city, on this miserable night!

Wait, who's that? Some poor guy with his wife on a donkey. She looks pregnant. On a night like this, with this crowd? They can't hardly get through the people. Must be looking for a place to stay. Good luck! Everything's taken. I watch them go from place to place. Everybody just shakes their head. No room.

They seem like a nice couple. Quiet. Especially the wife, not yelling at her husband like all the other women. She looks, well, patient. And he's looking at her with those big, warm eyes. Eyes like you've never seen before. Placid. Confident. At ease with himself and the world. Unlike everybody else in this miserable crowd.

Time to get to my room. The innkeepers are thieves. Jacked up the prices because they knew there would be a crowd. Funny, the inns are full and the shops are empty. All sold-out. Can't buy anything to eat or drink, all you can do is just grab a little water from the well.

If Caesar were here he'd be laughing at this mess. He knows how to get people riled up. You can feel it in the crowd. They press in on you, bumping, rudely yelling for you to get out of the way. And the noise, it's overwhelming. Can't they just shut up! My inn is no better. Might as well sleep in the street.

There's that guy again. Wandering through the crowd. What's he want? He looks a little frantic. Probably lost his wife in this mob.

"Please, sir. My wife just had a baby. She's thirsty. Can you spare a little water?"

A baby! On a night like this. So I give the kid a little of my water. He gives me a nod of thanks and walks away, back through the crowd.

But ... his eyes! They looked right through me. Big, trusting eyes. Full of love and compassion, and... This is crazy. In this crowd, this miserable crowd, to be thinking of eyes, and noticing eyes and how peaceful and loving they are.

What about that guy? Clean, but with big, calloused hands, like a tradesman. Maybe a carpenter. And, a baby, on a miserable night like this. There he is at the edge of the crowd. I think I'll follow him. See where he's going. Can't get to the inn, might as well see the new baby.

It's tough getting through the crowd, but I'm keeping my eyes on the carpenter as he weaves his way through the mass of people. They yell at him as he pushes his way through, polite, but determined to get to his wife with that small cup of water.

As we move on, the crowd begins to thin. The noise level is lower now. I can feel my pulse slowing as I see something in the distance. It looks like a little barn. Maybe that's where that pair ended up. And where the baby was born.

Animals are milling about, their breath steamy in the cool air. And, what's this? Shepherds. What are they doing here? No need to push my way through them. They stand aside, allowing me to get up close. There's a crowd here, too. But a different kind of crowd. Quiet. Respectful. Almost ... adoring. Some regal-looking characters stand off to the side, their arms filled with gifts for the child I guess.

Suddenly the carpenter looks my way. He smiles, and those eyes burn into mine. He nods to his wife, she looks up with even bigger eyes, more lovely and loving than any eyes I've ever seen. And she smiles. She knows! She knows I was the one who gave them water. I seem to have fallen on my knees. Why? It seems foolish for me to be on my knees. But then I notice that everyone else is also kneeling. The kings. The shepherds, even some of the animals.

Wait, there's something else. It's ... so ... calm. My breathing is quiet, almost contemplative. And, there's music. Rich, soaring, beautiful singing. A massive chorus. Where's it coming from? And what are they singing? ... "Glory to God in the highest ...And Peace..." Peace. I can feel it; it enwraps me.

The woman holds up the baby. He's looking right at me. His eyes more beautiful even than his mother's. His eyes hold mine and I'm speechless with wonder.

Somehow I know that because of this child, and this wonderful, glorious night, my life will never be the same. And the world itself will have been changed forever.

But, All is Not Well in Bethlehem

> "Go, and find out what you can about this child, and when you find him let me know so I also may go and adore him." Matthew 2.8

BEFORE LEAVING THE animal shelter where the baby was born, I resolved to try to follow this family to see what the child might grow up to be: If he would fulfill the expectations generated by the grandiose circumstances of his birth, or grow up to be just another good Jewish kid. I decided to write down my thoughts so I could remember them and maybe read them later. Perhaps other people might also want to read my Jesus Diary someday to learn more about him.

Through diligent snooping I soon found out that I had correctly judged that his father was a carpenter and that his name was Joseph. The mother, whose name was Mary, seemed very young. I also learned they had named the child Jesus. They appeared to be an ideal family, with great promise due to their quite obvious strong bonds of faith and love.

So it was with great pleasure in this new-found knowledge that I was in my room at the inn, basking in the remembrance of the warm and loving scene at the manger. I felt I had seen a miracle and was filled with excitement over this new child. But at that very moment dark shadows were forming elsewhere in town, hints of unheard of evil doings about to take place.

It seems that those well-dressed adorers at the stable where the child had been born actually were royalty who had traveled quite a distance, following a star they felt signified that this child was something very special. Perhaps even a king. I found that odd. Kings are born in palaces, amidst luxury and the best of care, not in a rustic lean-to surrounded by animals.

I overheard them saying that, out of courtesy, they had stopped to see King Herod to introduce themselves and discuss the reason for their journey. He seemed very interested, especially when they said that the star may be an omen that a new king is about to be born. "Well," he had said "when you find him let me know where he is so I can adore him too." They promised they would let him know on their way out of town.

I should have immediately known that something was amiss. Kings normally do not welcome competition. Unless Herod was a very strange monarch, I can't imagine that he was pleased with the news. However, it seems he kept his cool, but he must have been inwardly horrified at the very thought of a new king.

I think I had just fallen asleep when the madness began. The peacefulness of that night and my dreams were shattered with a riotous scene taking place outside my window. I heard horrible screams as people began to grasp what Herod had in mind as a response to the new king. From my window I could see women, and men too, running wildly about clutching their children in their arms in a frantic attempt to escape Herod's murderous forces. Thinking that I could somehow be of help, I rushed from my inn. What met my eyes when I reached the street was more horrible than anything I had ever seen. The cruelty was breathtaking.

There was blood everywhere. Armed soldiers were ripping infants from their parents' arms and slashing them ruthlessly with their swords. Once the child was dead they tossed the body to the ground with a diabolical casualness. According to Herod's edict no male child younger than two years of age was spared. From what I saw, I don't think those ravenous soldiers bothered to check the age of their prey. They went about it with a vengeance, following Herod's orders with fiendish enthusiasm. I was sick. I returned to my room in a daze.

But what about Jesus, the child in the manger with those wonderful, beautiful eyes? And his mother Mary, just a girl, and that staunch guy Joseph her husband? What happened to them? Did Herod's men get to them too? I now felt even more terrible than before, because I had seen those eyes, and they had seen me, and I had been moved like never before at the flood of love and compassion they instilled in me. Hatred of Herod flared up in my soul. If I had been one of his men I might have turned my sword against him instead of these poor harmless children. But soldiers are trained to follow orders, and so they did.

I barely slept another minute that night. Overwhelmed by grief, I left Bethlehem the very next day, hoping to remove the blood and grime of the place forever from my mind. What had begun as a crowded busy night in the city had been transformed into incredible bliss by the birth of a magical child.

And then, just as suddenly and unexpectedly, trauma exploded in my head as I saw the most incredible evil in the world played out before me. I wept with the realization that the hope that this new child's birth seemed to promise to the world was not to be. Because he was no more. Herod had won. He was still king.

I Was in Total Despair...

> And every year his parents went to Jerusalem for the solemn Passover days. And so they went according to their custom when he was twelve years old. Luke 2.41

... AT THE THOUGHT that I might never see these people again. Burdened with an indelible memory of the horrible slaughter of innocent children, I convinced myself that, for the sake of my own sanity, I should try to forget everything I felt and saw that fateful night in Bethlehem. It was unreal, yet it was very real indeed in that I saw it with my own eyes. But now it was over, done, and best forgotten.

But try as I might, I couldn't forget it. I returned home, frustrated and sad. A nagging mental itch ate at my mind, and I could not help asking the question: "Why?" Why was I the one person in that whole churning crowd that Joseph approached for water? Why couldn't I have just given him the water and forgotten about it? Why did the baby have to be born that very night and why was I so drawn to see him? Why was I singled out to be witness of this miraculous birth?

Was this supposed to be some omen for me, that I should amend my life? Was I to carry these memories with me forever, totally frustrated in my desire to know more about this mysterious family, and whether they lived or died, and if they lived, where? Was his blood spilled on that gory night, making my brief encounter with Jesus a cruel coincidence, without meaning or substance?

Somehow I believed that he had survived the massacre in Bethlehem, but I knew not how. The circumstances of his birth were simply too spectacular to be meaningless. I recalled the shepherds and the noble visitors from the east. I heard again the angelic choir singing "Peace on Earth." I relived the warmth and wonder of that miraculous night. It was too special to ever be erased from my memory.

As the years went by my belief grew stronger. The experience lived on in me. Convinced that he was alive, I tried to piece together a picture of what the early life of a boy named Jesus might be like. I mused that, since Joseph was a carpenter, he would probably be passing that trade on to his son, slowly developing his woodworking skills. Mary, as a young mother, was probably accomplished at all the skills young women needed to master: spinning, sewing, and of course, cooking for her family. I became enamored of this idyllic family, even though it existed only in my mind. I could see them going about their daily activities; I could feel the genuine warmth and love that they shared. I wished I could be part of it.

Several years later, I happened to be in a group traveling to Jerusalem for the holy days. It was quite a large caravan, made up of various families, tribes and villagers, all traveling together but still segmented within their own parties. Always eager to meet new people and on the lookout for my cherished family, I shuttled about from group to group. Every now and then a familiar face would pop into view, but not the ones I was looking for.

It was early spring, in the month of Nisan, and the area surrounding Jerusalem was abounding in beauty. The Redbud trees were in bloom, rabbits and other critters scurried about and doves and sparrows cooed and sang. The pilgrims also joined in song. As I wandered among the throng, however, I failed to see anyone who resembled Joseph and his family. We finally arrived in Jerusalem where, over the course of two days, the impressive Passover ceremonies at the temple were executed with perfection.

I started the return trip with a heavy heart. I was convinced that it would be in circumstances such as these that I would run across Jesus and his parents. There would be other opportunities, I was sure, but the sense of disappointment lingered. Just as my mood turned especially dark over some barking dogs that would not leave me alone, I thought I saw a familiar face in the distance. I was sure it was Joseph. I angled my way closer to him.

As I came within earshot, I heard anxious voices coming from the group surrounding Joseph. I could see Mary too, and she was crying. I wondered what could be wrong. I was overjoyed to see them, but they were not interested in talking to me.

"I thought he was with your group," Joseph said. "No, we thought he was with you," someone replied. "Well, he must be somewhere in this caravan," Joseph said. "Let's look around and see if we can find him."

I asked how old the boy was, presuming it must be Jesus who was lost. "About twelve," someone said. Twelve. Could it be that long since that unforgettable night? Snapping out of a brief reverie, I joined the others in their search for the lost Jesus. Soon the entire caravan was aware that a twelve year old boy was missing.

By nightfall, we still had not found him, so Mary and Joseph and a few kinsmen decided to return to Jerusalem the following day. Perhaps he was lost in that big and unfamiliar city. I was sad that Jesus was lost but filled with hope that at least he was alive. No one slept well that night.

I joined the group that set out at daybreak, back to the holy city and the temple. It had been three days since Jesus was lost and we all were concerned for his wellbeing. We thought he would know to go to the temple, sensing that he would be safe there and might even find a generous person to help him. We did not want to think of him wandering the streets, homeless and frightened.

The temple was eerily quiet after the hustle and bustle of the Passover festivities, yet we could hear a lively conversation taking place in a small alcove. There was an eager back and forth, as ideas were proposed, argued, and either amended or dropped. This was typical, as rabbis were constantly debating the laws and the prophecies.

We certainly were not expecting to see Jesus in the middle of this conversation. But there he was! Not just listening to the rabbis and asking them questions, but doing so with a level of confidence and knowledge far beyond what might be expected from a twelve year old.

Jesus had not gotten lost on the way home from observing the Passover. Nor had he been wandering around in tears as one might expect in such circumstances. No, he wasn't lost at all. Instead of joining up with the caravan heading for home, he had stayed behind in Jerusalem. Whether he had been invited to stay by one of the rabbis or decided to do so on his own, no one was sure. And he wasn't telling.

In fact, he seemed a little perturbed at our appearance. Distraught, Mary said "We've been looking for you for three days." Jesus' reply was a very nonchalant, "Why did you worry? Didn't you know I had to be tending to my Father's business?" I had no idea what his Father's business might be, but I thought that was not a polite way to talk to his mother. And how did Joseph feel? Isn't he his father? And isn't he a carpenter? What does that business have to do with the rabbis and the temple? We were all confused at his words. But, eventually the hurt feelings were soothed, and Jesus headed home with his parents, once more the quiet and dutiful son.

I became separated from them on the way home and did not get a chance to discuss this frightening occurrence with Jesus or his parents. But there was quite a bit of conversation about it among our fellow travelers. Not all had a high opinion of Jesus at this point, thinking he might be getting a little ahead of himself, and disappointed in the way he talked to his mother.

When we got home, I discovered that they lived on the opposite side of town. I couldn't keep daily tabs on Jesus but I could surely keep on top of local gossip and opinions of this precocious youngster.

From what I could glean from conversations with friends and acquaintances of the family, I learned that Jesus made rapid progress in anything he put his hand to. He was learning his trade well. He got along with the rest of the children in the neighborhood but was not especially popular. Some of the kids complained that he acted like he was already a rabbi, constantly advising them and telling them what to do.

For me, the entire experience was a phenomenal success. Jesus was alive. He was lost and had been found. But I still wondered over his comment about his father's business.

A Man Named John

> "I baptize with water but you do not know that there is one among you who will come after me, even though he was made before me, the strap of whose sandal I am not worthy to untie." John 1.26

THE YEARS WENT quickly, and due to pressure of business and family, I had lost touch with Jesus again. However, the memory of him and his parents remained etched in my mind. After all, who could forget such an amazing character? His miraculous birth and the slaughter that followed it; his obvious maturity and poise that allowed him to interact as an equal with learned men and rabbis; these are things one does not easily forget.

So I had increased my efforts to rediscover my lost Jesus but was not having much luck. I kept an alert ear to the ground at all times. Whenever there was word of a newcomer with promise or a unique event no one could explain I jumped at the opportunity to check it out, as those were the kind of situations where Jesus might show up. Unfortunately, most of these investigations were fruitless, but they were nevertheless interesting and fun.

One of the most enticing opportunities to find Jesus concerned a new prophet named John, who was preaching doom and gloom and urging repentance from sin. There were rumors that he lived alone in the wilderness like a hermit; that he ate wild and weird things, like grasshoppers and honey from wild bees. He talked of something he called "baptism." I wasn't sure what that was. But he was quite a topic of conversation so I thought I'd see what he was all about.

I first saw John at the river Jordan, where he was ranting about judgment and imminent perdition. Some people were taking it very seriously, but others were laughing and joking at his appearance and style. I tried to get up close so I could hear him better.

He certainly was a unique sight! He was wearing something that looked like the skin of an animal, not a normal robe or a toga like the Romans wear. I don't think he had bathed in weeks, if not years. But he looked healthy enough. Maybe all the bugs he was eating were more nourishing than I expected. He had a strong resonant voice that carried very well.

As I listened to him rage about how we were all sinners and needed to repent, a number of people approached him and asked him about this "baptism" he was talking about. Some of them wanted to try it, it seems, for they followed as he led them into the water. He dunked them underwater for just a few seconds and then said some words to them that I could not hear.

I found this all this very strange, but what came next knocked me off my feet. It happened so suddenly I almost didn't realize what was taking place before me. John's eyes sparkled with excitement and his voice became louder and faster. But then he seemed to calm down. Someone in the crowd had attracted his attention.

Obviously focused on the newcomer who had caught his eye, John explained that the baptism he was offering was just water, but that there would be another who would come and who would baptize with the "holy spirit." I didn't know what that meant. Then he shouted "Behold! The Lamb of God!"

Now I was truly confused. And even more so when John added "He takes away the sins of the world." Now I knew he was crazy. Some people started laughing. But they quickly quieted down as a handsome young man began walking slowly through the crowd, approaching John. It was Jesus!

I recognized him immediately. Sure, he was older, perhaps thirty or so, but there was something about his bearing that convinced me this was the same Jesus I had seen so many years ago. Maybe that irrepressible confident look on his face, and the same piercing eyes that I would never forget. He glanced my way as he passed and I think I detected a glimmer of recognition. Later I would understand that of course he knew who I was, because he knew everything. Jesus was coming to be baptized. By John.

They spoke quietly together as if they were relatives, which, I discovered much later, they were. Jesus was asking to be baptized and it seems John was reluctant. He said Jesus was the one who should be baptizing him! So why don't they just baptize each other, I thought.

But John continued calling Jesus the Lamb of God, and claiming that he takes away the sins of the world. This was getting confusing. What is a Lamb of God and what and whose sins is he taking away? And where is he taking them? These were entirely new concepts to me, and to the rest of the crowd it seemed, as there were a lot of quizzical looks among them.

For as long as anyone could remember, there had always been a promise of a Messiah, a savior, a great prophet who would appear in Israel and rebuild the nation that had once been a major world power. He would be a new king who would overthrow the Romans. It was a very popular concept and a great many people liked the idea of a strong powerful Israel. Was Jesus this Messiah, this king? If that was so then those strange men from the east were right. And so was Herod.

I could not believe my eyes and ears at what happened next. When Jesus stepped out of the water it seemed as if the very sky opened up and a bird, a large dove actually, came swiftly down and hovered right above Jesus. Meanwhile the earth shook with the sound of a deep, rich, mighty voice: "This is my beloved son. I am well pleased with him. Listen to him!" Just as suddenly, the skies closed and the bird was gone. But we all stood there, speechless.

If there had ever been any doubt in my mind that Jesus was something very special it was instantly wiped away by this earth-shaking event. People began talking about the experience. There was a palpable sense of excitement over it, over John, and especially over Jesus. I overheard someone say "We just saw the Messiah!" I quickly agreed.

When I was relaxing at home that night I tried to fathom what had happened. I could not get that miraculous voice out of my ears. It had called Jesus "my beloved son." Could this be the father Jesus was talking about many years ago in the temple in Jerusalem? Trying to figure out this riddle wore me out and I fell asleep in my chair.

Months later I learned that Herod, urged on by the Pharisees, had arrested John and held him in prison. John had publicly criticized Herod for marrying Herodias, his brother's wife. I think this would have been allowed and even encouraged under the old laws of Moses, but John said it was wrong. As a result, Herodias hated John and wanted him out of the way, but Herod kept resisting her demands. He liked talking to John and would visit him frequently in jail.

John's luck ran out at a party Herod hosted for some of the community leaders, at which Herodias and her daughter were present. Herod was so taken by the beauty of his wife's daughter that he promised he would give her anything she asked for. Prompted by Herodias, she immediately requested the head of John the Baptist on a platter.

Ashamed to go back on his promise, he had John executed that very day. To me, this seemed like a sickening way to honor a stupid vow made under the influence of alcohol and tantalizing youthful beauty. But that's the kind of person Herod was.

I Heard He Started a Club

> "Come, follow me, and I will make you fishers of men." Mark 1.16

THE NEWS OF the extraordinary events at the Jordan River spread quickly throughout the area. Of course, everybody had an opinion. Some said it was a group-dynamic mental breakdown, and that people just thought they heard those booming words from the sky. They said the bird itself was nothing special. There are a lot of doves in the area during this time of the year.

These explanations seemed a little too glib for me. There was so much that happened that afternoon at the river that it would be easy for someone to get hung up on just one aspect and fail to grasp the totality of what took place. For how often does one run across a character like John, with his camel skin outfit and porridge of locusts and wild honey?

And no one had ever experienced a weather phenomenon such as had taken place here, with the skies opening up so dramatically. And then the thunderous clamor from the heavens basically identifying this man Jesus as the Son of God! Even the bird was special. It wasn't just a dove. It didn't look like a dove and didn't act like a dove. Doves avoid people, but this one hovered over Jesus like a protective shield. The whole experience was unreal.

But I knew it was real. Because I saw it with my own eyes and because I knew who Jesus was. I had always known; from the very first moment I saw him, I knew he was special. But now I found myself asking just how special was he? Was he special enough to be that king that the old timers always talked about in the synagogue? That Messiah they had been hoping for, as they said, "from ages?" Well if what I saw at the Jordan was real he certainly had all the qualifications to be the savior who would rebuild Israel.

Evidently he stirred up as much confidence in some of the other folks as he did in me. For I heard later on that a certain number of guys in the crowd had pledged themselves to him to help him advance his promise for the country. He was starting a club.

They were fishermen. A couple of them, Simon and his brother Andrew, were angling in the Sea of Galilee one day when Jesus saw them and made them a most interesting offer, by suggesting they might accomplish more in life by joining him and becoming fishers of men. Two other fishermen named James and John, who were the sons of Zebedee, also joined him, leaving their father right there, sitting alone in the boat, while they walked off with Jesus. That was the type of power he radiated. They were his gang and they were going to learn from him and help spread his ideas.

Maybe other guys besides fishermen would join up with him someday. Maybe I would be one of them.

It Was the Strangest Wedding I Ever Attended...

"Everybody first puts out the good wine, and, when the guests have become tipsy, that which is lesser quality. You, however, have saved the good wine until now!" John 2.10

I THINK THE NEXT time Jesus became big news was over the incident at the wedding feast at a town called Cana. He, his mother, and some of his followers had been invited to the celebration. I don't know why Joseph wasn't there; maybe he had a job to finish in his carpenter shop.

I also knew the family, so I was there with some of my friends. We all planned to have a good time, for the wedding couple were known to be very generous hosts, serving plenty of delicious food and wine of excellent quality.

I didn't know ahead of time that Jesus would be there. I hadn't been hearing much about him lately. Maybe he was lying low because a couple of his friends were known to become a little overly enthusiastic at times. Simon especially, was a well-known hothead with quite a reputation for outlandish statements and behavior. But I was glad to see that Jesus was invited and I hoped to get a chance to talk to him. Perhaps I also could join up and become a fisher of men.

The ceremony was perfectly executed under the most stringent rabbinical standards. The bride was radiant; the groom stately and handsome. Moms cried, the musicians played, we all danced the Hora, the food was set forth, and the wine poured. We had just raised the first toast. And the wine was good, very good.

But I had noticed when I first entered the dining hall that there was a certain odd tension in the room. What could be wrong, I thought? Everything was perfect, so far, and the hosts were known for their partying and party-giving skills. Maybe it was just me, over excited at the thought of seeing my Jesus again and maybe even getting to be one of his men.

The tension in the room soon exploded into a full-blown controversy. The rumor spreading across the room made no sense. They have run out of wine? Already, with just the first toast gone down? How is that even possible? If there had been a wine merchant in the crowd at that moment I think he would have been killed.

The argument that ensued was most frightening to behold. "You didn't order enough!" "Yes, I did!" I thought I was listening to kids fighting on a playground. The yelling and cursing went on for hours, it seemed, although it was actually only about fifteen minutes. Whether the merchant was short on his shipment or the shipment was hijacked on the road to Cana was never determined. But the voices were rising and the threat of violence was in the air. The bride was in tears; the brave groom tried to comfort her while glancing menacingly at the wine steward.

A soft, gentle voice soon quieted the crowd. It was Mary, the mother of Jesus! Evidently she had a plan to solve this catastrophe. She was walking toward her son, who was sitting in a corner laughing and joking with some of his buddies. He hadn't noticed that the wine had run out and was oblivious to all the fighting. Maybe Mary had some wine at home and was going to ask Jesus to go and get it. Just like a mom, she was always trying to solve everybody's problem. Jesus and his pals could certainly find some wine somewhere and salvage this party.

Mary approached Jesus and told him about the shortage of wine. We all figured he would hop up right away and do something about it. After all, she is his mother. But, his response astounded us. He basically told her it was of no concern to him and she should not worry about it. But she just looked at him in that way that only moms can look at their sons, and confidently said to the wine steward "Do whatever he tells you." I think I detected a twinkle in her eye. Jesus did not disappoint her, but rose to the occasion in spectacular style.

Murmuring and quizzical looks abounded as the crowd pondered what Jesus was going to do to get a sufficient quantity of potable wine for so many people. Nobody had a clue; but Jesus had it all figured out. As was usual in a Jewish wedding there were a number of large vessels for washing up before dinner. "Fill those jars with water," he told the wine steward. And so he did, all six of them. These were quite large jars, each holding about twenty gallons.

After the jars were filled as Jesus had instructed, he walked over to them, dipped his finger in one and nodded in approval. There was an audible gasp as we all noticed his fingertip was purple.

"Now let the steward taste it," he said. A large ladle was brought forth and dipped into one of the jars. There was a lot of anxious twittering going on among the wedding guests, for the thought of no more wine was frightening. If Jesus didn't come through for them now the party was over.

The steward lifted the ladle carefully, raised it so he could sniff its aroma, rolled his eyes, and sipped a bit of what now looked to be wine. His eyes widened, a smile beamed on his face, and he uttered a single word. "Wow!"

The crowd erupted in applause. He had done it! Jesus quietly walked away, rejoining his friends. His mother smiled. The wine flowed freely and did not run out again. Before I knew it I had had my fill of this excellent wine and was starting to feel a little woozy.

All too soon the party was over, and I never did get a chance to talk to Jesus.

At the Temple

> The Chief Priests and the Scribes sought how they could destroy him, for they were afraid of him because the whole world was enthralled with his teaching.
> Mark 11.18

WORD OF THIS miraculous production of an excellent vintage wine spread quickly throughout the town of Cana. I think Jesus was a little embarrassed by the sudden notoriety and decided to stay out of the spotlight for awhile. He and his gang moved on, and I knew not where.

Some time later, I, along with thousands of other pilgrims, traveled to Jerusalem to celebrate the Passover. It's always a big occasion, and draws massive crowds from all over the country. Although there are always many individual parties and gatherings, the main events take place at the temple.

Now, everyone knows that the temple in Jerusalem is a very sacred and revered place. This is where the High Holy Days are commemorated; where the High Priest officiates; and where people from all walks of life come to offer sacrifice. It's also where many of them get fleeced.

It's a busy place, a madhouse, sometimes. There is so much going on it's almost like a carnival, with animals, holy men, and visitors from all across the land. Also shysters and crooks.

When pious folks from the countryside arrive in the big city they immediately become targets for some of the shadier characters in town. It's always necessary to watch one's money bag very closely. Not just for light-fingered pick pockets, but even more so for the crooked moneychangers in the temple itself.

And it was at the temple that I next saw Jesus. And heard him, too! He was there, along with a couple of his special fishers of men; they were taking in the crowds and the scenery, the same as the rest of the folks.

And, there was a lot to see. It may be a temple, and a holy place, but on that particular day it seemed more like a barn. Livestock were all over the place: sheep, oxen, goats; and birds, pigeons and doves of all colors. Some were in pens and cages, but many were just wandering around, accompanied by their owners who were offering them for sale as sacrifice. I didn't hear the prices, but I bet they were outrageous.

The noise, the bleating of lambs, the moaning of oxen, and cooing of doves and pigeons filled the air. Unfortunately the air was also filled with the odors of these animals and their droppings. It hardly seemed to be a holy place. Adding to the din was the incessant hawking and yelling of the vendors of these animals. It was as if Yahweh would be stirred into action on your behalf because you bought a goat from Ahab, instead of his rival Jeddah. Some of the backwoodsmen fell for this salesmanship and willingly emptied their purses for a favored animal.

Visitors often had to exchange their funds from their local currency into the denomination required by the temple authorities before purchasing their sacrificial animals. Thus, the moneychangers were there for their convenience.

They had set up their booths and were busily exchanging odd monies from the provinces for the proper funds for use in the temple, exacting a fee, of course, for the transaction. Since some of their customers were totally unfamiliar with the money they were given, the moneychangers could charge whatever they could get away with. There was no accounting, no oversight; it was an opportunity for graft and greed.

Local folks knew the game, and complained lustily when the numbers didn't add up. Even the sharpest of shysters were frustrated in their attempts to shortchange them. But few out-of-towners complained, mainly because they were unfamiliar with the money and the exchange process itself. There were often language problems as well. And many were simply terrified just being in the big city and were afraid to raise a ruckus.

As I was taking this all in and smiling inwardly at some of the more outrageous heists being perpetrated in broad daylight, I spotted Jesus and, I think, John, his newest and youngest disciple. They were taking it in as well, and Jesus did not look happy.

I'm not sure what set him off, but all of a sudden he strode up to the area where the animals and their tenders were congregated. He had fashioned a sort of cat-o-nine-tails out of some cord and was thrashing it about menacingly, his eyes ablaze as he marched onward.

What is he doing? What has come over him? At the wedding feast he had seemed like a nice, quiet sort of guy, meek and humble even after pumping out a hundred and twenty gallons of top-quality wine. But what I saw before me now was a different person entirely. There was a ferocity in his manner that made me shiver. He cracked his whip above his head and shouted "Get Out!"

The animals started running in all directions. He prodded them with the whip. They crashed through the doors of the Temple and ran free in the courtyard. They, at least, would not be sacrificed tonight.

Then he turned on the sellers of the beasts, the hawkers and salesmen, the greedy purveyors of sacrificial meat. His whip cracked again, and they almost fell over each other in their haste to avoid feeling its sting. The look on their faces was one of sheer terror. They were not used to such treatment, but they did not stand there to complain about it. They turned tail and ran.

Then it was the moneychangers' turn. I could tell they were frozen in fear as he approached, his whip cracking again. He chased them out before they could grab the money from their counting tables. In fact, he flipped their tables over, all their drachmas, shekels, and denarii cascading to the floor, rolling around like little wheels.

Some children scurried about, scooping up the coins and hiding them in their cloaks, looking around with guilty faces to check if anyone saw them.

At the fleeing moneychangers Jesus shouted, "Get out! This isn't a marketplace!" And, then he added: "This is my Father's house!"

Wait a minute, I thought. It's one thing to kick people and animals out of the temple, but it's quite something else to say that Yahweh is your father, and, as this is his house, that therefore you are his son. Was Jesus really saying that? Is that what I heard?

As I was trying to make sense out of this complex choice of words, some of the priests came running up to Jesus and shouted "Just who do you think you are?" "Where do you get the authority to kick these people out and turn over their counting tables?" He had indeed made a large mess of the place and they were justifiably angry.

But now he really confused me. He told them that he could not only make a mess if he wanted to but he could knock down the whole temple and then rebuild it in just three days. I had no idea what that meant. But he was a carpenter, and I suppose a good one. But, three days? What was he talking about?

So it was not just his actions, bizarre as they were, that astonished me on this crazy day, but it was what he said after he finished causing mayhem, and what his words implied. Jesus was getting more and more mysterious by the minute.

I left the Temple with his words ringing in my ears. This was not the first time I heard him called the Son of God. Things were starting to make sense to me and I couldn't wait to learn more.

The Son of God?

> "He who believes in him will not be judged; however he who does not believe is already judged, because he did not believe in the name of the only-begotten Son of God." John 3.18

I SPENT QUITE A bit of time pondering what Jesus had said. Is it possible that he could be the Son of God?

I knew that the gods and goddesses of the Romans and Greeks often had children, sometimes by highly unusual means. One Greek god, Athena, I believe, came into being by popping out of Zeus' forehead after he had swallowed her mother Metis. That, I thought, was ridiculous. Nevertheless, because the Greeks already had so many gods, some of whom had sons and daughters, and even wives, I thought they might welcome Jesus as the Son of God into their Pantheon.

And, as Romulus and Remus, the founders of the city of Rome, were believed to be sons of the god they called Mars, I thought they also might welcome Jesus as the Son of another God.

If you counted the number of Roman gods and goddess you would have to conclude that they were very religious people. The gods ruled their lives. The months of their year were all named after a god. They even had a god of the new year, called Janus, who had two faces so he could look backward and forward at the same time.

Many Roman homes had a shrine devoted to special household gods, including the Lares, who watched over the house itself, and another group, called Penates, who assured that there was adequate food and drink in the pantry. On special occasions, like weddings and birthdays, devout Romans would make offerings to these household gods.

The Romans attributed the success of their city and their empire to the depth of their piety. In fact, I had heard that, not too many years before Jesus was born, they had begun making their deceased emperors into gods. This deification process began with Julius Caesar and I believe was still ongoing.

I thought for these reasons that the Romans would eagerly welcome Jesus. They were always looking to their gods for help, so why not add another one, especially one that had the powers that Jesus exhibited. He seemed so powerful that any sensible Roman would want to add him to his divine inventory.

I don't think they would like the idea of just one God, though. If they decided to worship the God of Jesus, what would happen to all their other gods? Many of them had distinct human qualities, and were known to become quarrelsome if not properly adored. They would not take kindly to another god, no matter how powerful, who might make them obsolete.

The same issue complicated life between the Jews and Romans. The Hebrews were monotheistic. We were taught that there was only one God, and he was Yahweh. He was fearsome and unforgiving. He demanded to be worshiped in specific ways. We have had a complicated relationship with our God. He has always been doing things for us, like rescuing us from Egypt, producing manna in the desert, sending plagues against our enemies, but people kept turning their backs on him. There have been several agreements, called covenants, between Yahweh and his people, over the years, and the way things are going now, it's probably time for a new one.

At one point, angered by mankind's infidelity and ingratitude, Yahweh decided to do away with the whole human race by sending a giant flood to drown them all. Fortunately a few survived, thanks to a legendary prophet and ship builder named Noah, who convinced God to give them another chance. I wasn't sure if the flood story was real, but, based on what I saw going on in the world, I wouldn't blame Yahweh for being upset with what humanity has become.

The Pharisees were doing their part to try to set things right with Yahweh by dictating how he should be worshiped and making sure all the laws and regulations were strictly observed. They were the sole interpreters of hundreds of rules affecting virtually every aspect of one's life, from ritualistic hand washing to what and when to eat and what can and cannot be done on the Sabbath. I personally thought they made up some of these rules, although they maintained they were just following the dictates of the prophets and the ancient writings.

However, I had to admit, although I was no expert, I had never heard or read about Yahweh having a son. I wondered, if Jesus really were the Son of God, is it possible he was sent here to patch things up between Yahweh and his people?

This was getting too complicated for me, but, I thought, if it were possible to repair the relationship between God and man, then Jesus would be just the person to do it.

The Woman at the Well

> And Jesus was tired from all his travels, so he sat down near the well. It was about noon. John 4.6

ONE DAY I overheard some women talking as they were busily looking for bargains in the market. There were the usual complaints about outrageous prices and scarcity of some essential household items. A good day at the market often meant a nice enjoyable evening at home, with fresh meats and vegetables and a cup or two of wine.

Shopping day also meant a stop at the town well for fresh water. The well was often an informal meeting place where neighborhood opinions and gossip were exchanged.

The women I was listening to had heard of a strange occurrence at the well in a town called Sichar, in Samaria. As I overheard them I slowly became convinced that my friend Jesus played a role in it.

The woman in question was a Samaritan, a group that was not especially popular with the Israelites. The well in Sichar was quite famous, for it was in an area that Jacob had given to his son Joseph, thus it was called Jacob's Well.

When she approached the well to draw some water, she was surprised to find a strange man sitting there. As he did not appear to have a rope or pail to draw water for himself, he asked her if he could have some of hers to drink.

She seemed surprised that a Jew would ask a Samaritan for water, since the two do not get along. But then the man said something curious. He said that, if she knew who he was, she would be the one asking him for water. And not normal water coming out of a well, but, as he put it, "living water."

This was starting to sound a lot like Jesus. And even more so when he explained how his water was different from what she was getting out of the well.

"If you drink this water you will get thirsty again, but you will never thirst again if you drink the water I have for you. It will give you everlasting life." She was astounded, and called him a prophet. "I want some of this water," she said.

Everlasting life? I staggered when I heard those words. I listened even closer as the women continued on with their gossip, saying that the man proceeded to tell this woman everything about her and her family in quite vivid detail. It was then that I knew it had to be Jesus.

Before the group at the well broke up to go back to their homes, one of the women recalled that the Samaritan said she told Jesus that she knew someday there was going to be a great prophet, a savior, a Messiah, and this person would be called the Christ.

His response blew me away: "I am the one" is what he said.

She later told her friends in Sichar about her experience. A lot of the Samaritans wanted to come and see this new prophet. And who could blame them? Who wouldn't want to know more about such an amazing man, who knew the deep dark secrets of peoples' lives and promised them an ever-refreshing drink that would not only quench their thirst but would bring them eternal life?

There was only one person in the world who could talk that way: Jesus, the self-proclaimed Son of God, the Christ.

A Long-Distance Miracle

> The man had faith in what Jesus told him and he went on his way. He believed in him, and so did his whole family. John 4.50,53

WORD OF THE marvelous deeds of Jesus, the carpenter turned prophet, spread rapidly thanks to multiple mouths willing to talk and an even greater number of ears equally willing to listen. Rumors flew about as creative minds conjured up more and more instances of the extraordinary doings of the Christ. Many were pure fantasy and hoax dreamt up by people seeking a sense of excitement in their boring lives. But some were true.

One event that expanded Jesus' notoriety concerned a well known royal official in Cana, the site of Jesus' first miracle. The man happened to be a friend of mine, and he related the incident for me with great enthusiasm. He said that he was excited when he heard Jesus was nearby and rushed to meet him. He desperately needed his help.

His son was near death in a neighboring town called Capharnaum, and he begged Jesus to go there with him to see if he could help him. He had heard of Jesus' reputation and he was convinced he could heal his son. He pleaded with Jesus to make the trip. Without even enquiring as to the nature of the boy's ailment, Jesus said he wouldn't go.

Not surprisingly, my friend was upset, and I guess, so was I, because I knew the young man and liked him. The official asked why couldn't Jesus at least go and see his son and find out what he could do about his illness, for the boy was at death's door. He begged him to change his mind and go with him to Capharnaum immediately.

But Jesus was unmoved by the father's passionate entreaty. He merely said, "Relax, your son is alive. Go see him." I couldn't believe it! Neither could my friend. But he took off for his son's bedside, full of hope yet not totally free of doubt. Jesus said his son was alive, but he hadn't even gone to see him. Was this a trick? If so, it was a cruel joke. Or, could it be…true? I followed along to see for myself.

My friend learned the truth as he was rushing to Capharnaum. In the distance, he saw a group of people coming towards him. He recognized them as some of his son's friends. His face fell. "They're probably coming to tell me he's already dead."

But as they got closer he heard them shouting and cheering at the top of their lungs. "He's alive and well" they called out to him. "Here he is!" they shouted. And my friend knew it was true when he saw his son in the very middle of the group, surrounded by his friends and full of smiles and good health. He was beside himself with happiness and relief, and squeezed his son in a warm fatherly embrace.

"When did you start to feel better?" he asked him. "Father, the fever broke a little after noon," was the reply. He knew that was the exact time when Jesus had told him his son was alive. "I should never have doubted him," he said, with a sheepish look on his face. But soon he was all smiles again, and so was everyone else, including me.

At Sheepgate Pond

> The man did not know the name of the person who had cured him, for Jesus had disappeared from the crowd that was in that place. John 5.13

I HAD HEARD OF a miraculous pond in Jerusalem near what is called Sheepgate. It had been reported that many cures took place there so I decided to go and see for myself. It sounded like the sort of place where Jesus might show up and I was hoping to see him. I was not disappointed.

The story of this particular healing pool is unique. According to local legend this is how it operates: the water in the pond is generally very still and placid. The ill and the aged and the crippled congregate around it with an intense look of expectation in their eyes. They are looking for the slightest rippling in the water, the merest disturbance of the tranquil surface of the pond.

It is said that the cause of the rippling of the water is due to an angel of the Lord coming down and stirring up the waters. When that happens the excitement begins, for the first person to enter the pond after the angel appears will be cured of whatever ails him. But not the second, or the third, or any of the other supplicants. Only the first.

There appears to be no set schedule for the angel to appear. It is totally random, thus making the hopefuls surrounding the pond very watchful and intent. Although there have been many miraculous cures here, many go on their way disappointed if they were not quick enough to plunge into the waters before anybody else.

When I arrived at the pond I was amazed at what I saw. I never knew there were so many aged and infirm people in Jerusalem, for the area around the pond was packed with people, some standing alone, others with an entourage to help carry them to the water when the time came. There was some jostling about as people tried to get in a top spot for a quick move to the water. But mostly it was calm and peaceful.

Some people were laughing and joking; a few kids were chasing each other and playing. But overall there was eager anticipation. I could feel it.

But then. Was that a flicker of disturbance on the water? There was a sudden stillness in the air, as people stopped what they were doing or saying and stared at the water. Did it or not? Yes! It moved! Then the surge began.

To be honest, it was hardly a surge. Nobody actually raced into the water after the angel disturbed it. Sick and old people do not move very fast. But they tried. They tried very hard. Some hobbled on one leg with a cane for support. Some crawled. Others, lying on their cots, had no chance at all, unless someone dragged or carried them to the water. The blind were totally out of luck, yet hopeful despite their long odds. My heart went out to them, all of them.

In a sense, it was pathetic. All these people, hundreds of them, had spent days and even weeks here, in the off chance that they might be fortunate enough to get to the pond before anyone else. And now I saw one lucky man actually do it!

It was a man with a withered arm who was first this time. After reaching the water he yelped with delight as his arm regained its normal shape and strength. He flexed his muscles a few times to see if it was really fixed, and a wide grin confirmed that it was.

Then he fell on his knees, as his family and friends crowded around him, jumping and shouting congratulations. He was a very happy man; and there would be a big party in his house tonight. Now, for once, he could be the perfect host, serving his guests food and drink with two good arms.

But the rest of the crowd was not so elated. They had failed again, some of them for the umpteenth time. A few continued to stare at the pond, praying that the angel was still available. But their eyes were empty of hope. Most just wagged their heads and slowly turned away. They would try again another day.

There were a few who seemed like they weren't going to move. They weren't going to take the chance to be absent when the angel came calling again. "When would it be?" was the question on everyone's mind. Five minutes? An hour? Or a matter of days or weeks? It didn't matter; just the chance for a cure drew people to the water's edge, regardless of how remote that chance might be.

I was in awe at the strong faith such people must have. How many times could a person come here hoping to be cured only to return home still ailing, but always ready to come again?

One such hopeful was an elderly man who seemed perfectly immobile on his cot. I couldn't imagine how he got there, unless some friends brought him. If so, it seems they had abandoned him now, as he was quite helpless. There were a few people around him offering some help. But, realistically what could they do?

Then Jesus came on the scene. He had been watching all along, I guess. The crowd of people parted as he walked up to the man on his cot. "Do you want to be cured?" he asked him.

I thought to myself: "What a question! Of course he wants to be cured! Why do you think he was here to begin with?" I was a little worried when Jesus didn't immediately go to Capharnaum to cure my friend's son; now I was very worried that he was not taking this poor man seriously. Was Jesus joking?

"Sir," the man said, lying prone on his bed, "I have been like this for thirty eight years! But there is nothing I can do. I can't walk. When the waters are disturbed there is no one to drag me to the pond. But I stay here because I believe that someday I can be cured." Jesus stared at the man and it was quite obvious he was moved by his faith.

Everyone was speechless, including me, even though I had been so eager at the chance to see Jesus again and maybe even talk to him. Thirty eight years! A lifetime, yet the man still believed he had a chance to be made whole. His faith was overwhelming.

We all looked at Jesus. What would he do? What could he do? Would he carry the man to the water all by himself and command the angel to appear again? He said he was the Son of God so I suppose he could have done it.

Instead, Jesus reached down to the man still flat on his cot and touched him lightly on the shoulder. Then, quite casually, he said "Get up. Pick up your cot and go home."

What? Did I hear that right? No one spoke. Not even the broken man on the cot. Then as if some unique serum began coursing through his veins, he began, slowly, ever so slowly, to get to his feet! The crowd went wild!

The man got up, hopped about a little to check out his newly cured legs, and then fell on his knees before Jesus, thanking him with an intensity that brought tears to my eyes. Jesus smiled at his enthusiasm. Thirty eight years of faith had finally been rewarded.

News of this miracle spread like wildfire. Jesus was instantly the talk of the town. He said he was the Son of God and he sure acted like it. Nobody ever did the kind of things he was doing, and with such a high level of confidence and self-assurance.

All Jerusalem was talking about him. But not all were happy with him.

The Backlash Begins

> "You scrutinize the scriptures because you think you will find eternal life in them. But they are all about me, and you do not wish to come to me so you may have life." John 5.39

DURING THE COURSE of the celebration, and unnoticed by me, Jesus had slipped away quietly, melting into the crowd as he so often did. People were so excited to see the helpless thirty-eight-year veteran of Sheepgate cured that they took no notice of his disappearance.

But there were other folks in the audience who were not celebrating the man's miraculous new mobility. In fact, they pulled him aside and started berating him for carrying the mattress he had been laying on when Jesus cured him. These were the Pharisees, a bunch of local leaders who had taken it upon themselves to see to the enforcement of the thousands of laws the Jewish people had to obey.

The laws were quite complex and detailed. It took an expert to figure them all out. I don't think anyone really understood them all, but there were some with which almost everyone was familiar: for instance, the laws covering what can and can't be done on the Sabbath.

The Sabbath was considered a day of rest. Tradition held that the Lord God himself rested on the Sabbath, having created the world and all that was in it in the previous six days and having seen that it was all very good.

But it was on the Sabbath that Jesus had cured this man. That, in itself, was of questionable legality. It could be argued that curing someone on the Sabbath was a violation of the law because it was a form of work, and work of any kind was forbidden on that day of rest.

On the other hand it could also be argued that it was not only allowed, but encouraged, as it was a good deed, something that should be done for the benefit of another person regardless of what day it was.

But, irrespective of the various opinions about the legality of Jesus curing the man, the Sabbath law was quite clear with regard to what this man was doing right now. He was carrying something! That it was his former cot made no difference. According to the law, one could only walk a certain distance on the Sabbath, beyond which it was a violation. But this man was not only walking but carrying his bed. That was definitely work, and therefore unacceptable and sinful.

They asked him "What do you think you're doing?" He said he was only doing what the man who had just cured him told him to do: "Get up, walk, carry your mattress." They wanted to know the name of this man who had cured him and told him to get up and walk, but nobody had any idea who he was. They started searching for him but he was nowhere to be seen, having slipped away in the excitement over the man's miraculous cure.

Once again I had hoped to talk to Jesus but he disappeared before I had a chance to do so. I was beginning to think he didn't like me following him around.

While standing there feeling sorry for myself, I overheard these petty officials talking about Jesus. They were outraged. They were of the opinion that curing on the Sabbath was illegal, and therefore he had broken the law. But even that wasn't the main reason they were irate.

He was ignoring them; worse than that, he was confronting them; he was making them look like fools. Their sense of powerlessness over this man blinded their sense of reality. They were mad at the good work he had done because, in doing so, he made them look bad.

They raged throughout the town hoping to find him and confront him, but he was nowhere to be found. Just as soon as there was word that he had been seen in a certain place, they scurried to it like little mice on the hunt for cheese. But, time after time, they were frustrated in their search. He always seemed just one step ahead of them, out of their reach.

Eventually they did meet up face to face, near the Sheepgate pond itself. Fortunately I had tagged along on some of their searches and was standing nearby when the confrontation began. Needless to say, it was no contest. If Jesus was capable of curing a youngster he had never seen and making this crippled man walk again, I thought he certainly could handle this posse of petty curmudgeons. Once again, I was not disappointed.

It started out with the usual hostility people often exhibit when their egos are challenged: Who do you think you are; and who says you can do this stuff; and don't you realize who we are and what we can do to you? All these hostile questions came flying at Jesus all at once, it seemed. Yet he was his usual calm self. I think he was looking forward to this duel.

I'd like to say I saw a glimmer of humor in his eyes, but it was really more like a smile of extreme self-confidence. He could handle anything. He was ready.

"Look," he told them: "I'm only doing what my Father is telling me to do. He's always working so it's only right that I should do the same. Your silly rules about the Sabbath are not my rules, nor my Father's. For he is busy right now maintaining his creation in existence. So don't try to tell me what I can and can't do and when."

No one had ever spoken to them like this.

But he was just getting started. He said: "All the power I have comes from my Father. In fact, you really haven't even begun to experience some of the truly astonishing things he can do. Whatever I do is because of him. If I raise people from the dead it's only because my Father does the same and wills me to do it. The day will come when all men will be raised up again, to be judged by their deeds. A good life will merit eternal life while evildoers will warrant condemnation. My Father has given me the power to exercise this judgment."

They were speechless. And mad.

But he kept on: "You hypocrites! You pretend to love God and follow his laws but you have no love in your hearts. My Father has sent me to you and you question everything I do instead of welcoming me as someone who can help you and improve your lives. You make great efforts to achieve glory before men but are unconcerned about the real glory that comes from loving and serving God. You study the scriptures and the law thinking that they can bring you life everlasting, but you're not willing to come to me for life."

When Jesus was finished, he looked around as if to see if there were any more questions. There were none. But there was much grumbling over his words and what they meant. If I heard him correctly, he had said that he could do work on the Sabbath because his Father also did so; that he was the Son of God; that he did all his good works because of his Father, and that he would judge all men. Including them!

It was from that point on that they began a concerted effort to catch him in some transgression that would allow the authorities to arrest Jesus and bring him to trial. I overheard some of the schemes that they were considering and they made me sick. Sick over the foolishness and pride of men. Self-destructive men who couldn't see their salvation right before their face.

He was offering them eternal life, and they wanted to put him to death.

The Sabbath Revisited

> And they were watching him to see if he world work some cure on the Sabbath, so that they could accuse him. Mark 3.2

ON ANOTHER OCCASION the legality of curing on the Sabbath was put to Jesus more directly.

While in the synagogue one Sabbath afternoon he came upon a man deeply in prayer. I also was there praying, but not so deeply that I failed to notice Jesus and a few of his disciples as they entered. I'm not sure that the devout man even saw Jesus or knew who he was. But Jesus noticed that one of the man's hands hung limp and useless at his side. It was severely withered and shrunken to about half of its normal size.

I didn't know what caused abnormalities like that, but the Pharisees were certain it was due to sin. I doubted that, because, if that were the case, I would be the most withered and abnormal person on earth. I was well aware of my past sins, which was why I was in the synagogue that very day.

I was also aware that Jesus and his followers were not alone, and that there was a small coterie of Pharisees who had quietly sneaked into the synagogue just after Jesus and his team had entered. It was well known that they had arranged to have him constantly followed wherever he went, so they could trap him in some misdeed.

This "tail" delegation was not very effective because it was made up of very poor sleuths who could not conceal their hatred and disdain for the one they were following. They were so obvious that there was no way Jesus or one of his men would fail to recognize them. This always gave Jesus the upper hand for any tricks or riddles they had planned to spring on him.

So, the stage was set for a confrontation. As the man remained deep in prayer he did not approach Jesus begging to be cured, as most ailing people would. Jesus was always being accosted by the blind and lame and leprous. But this man remained concentrated in his devotion and unaware of his surroundings.

Jesus did not wait for the man to notice him. Instead he went right up to him, tapped him on the shoulder and asked him if he could look at his hand. The man reacted with eagerness, sensing the potential for a cure. He stretched out his arm and opened his hand so Jesus could take a look at it. I must say it was a most pitiable sight.

The reaction of the Pharisaical "tail" was quite the opposite. They looked at each other with eyes that said "What's he planning to do now," and "I think we got him." According to their legalistic minds, if he cured this man on the Sabbath he would be in violation of the law and they could nail him for it.

Sure enough, Jesus asked the man if he would like his hand repaired. "Sir," the man said, "I don't know who you are, but if you can make it normal again, I beg you to do so." He knelt before Jesus.

I thought Jesus would, right then and there, make the man's hand perfect again and get on with his day. But no, he had something else in mind. Instead of fixing the man's hand he turned around and faced the bunch of Pharisees with raised eyebrows, and accosted them with: "Is it legal to do an act of kindness on the Sabbath?" They were smug and silent.

Then he said, "If I do not help this man, am I not actually harming him by failing to act on his behalf? Would not my inaction itself be sinful?" They seemed puzzled at the question, but still didn't say anything. Jesus looked at them with fire in his eyes.

Then he turned back to the man and demanded "Hold out your arm!" The man did so, and his hand was immediately restored. Frightened by the tension in the room, he backed away, bowing and thanking Jesus, but keeping a wary eye on everybody else. I think he was happy to get out of the synagogue that day.

Jesus looked at the Pharisee gang again, and one could easily tell he was upset. "You followed me here today not to come and pray, but to try to trap me in some devious scheme of yours. Why? Are your hearts so hard that you can attempt to use the Sabbath itself as a cause for condemnation of my good works?" Their guilty glances confirmed that they knew he was on to their game and had caught them again.

"Please listen and try to understand. It is essential to do good for another when the opportunity presents itself. Conversely, to fail to do what you can to help someone is in itself a transgression. To fail to do good when you can is to do harm. It's that simple. Whether it is the Sabbath or not is irrelevant. Would you actually want me to ask that poor man to come back again tomorrow so I can cure him? Would that make you happy?"

They remained speechless. I had never seen a group of well-educated Pharisees so dumbfounded. I kept quiet too, secretly enjoying the bind he had put them in. There was no way they could get out of this without looking insensitive and even cruel.

"Let me put it this way," Jesus said, "The Sabbath was made for man, not man for the Sabbath." Then he added, "And I have authority over the Sabbath."

I can only imagine the discussion that took place among that group of amateur sleuths when they returned to their lair. Defeated and embarrassed once again, they would nevertheless keep trying.

But Jesus made it clear to them that the Sabbath was just like any other day so far as he and his Father were concerned, and they would have to come up with better schemes than this if they hoped to ever outsmart him.

Razing the Roof

> They were completely shocked, and they glorified God, saying: "We have indeed seen some miraculous things today!" Luke 5:26

AFTER THESE EVENTS, there was no stopping Jesus as he went about proving time and time again that he was indeed the Son of God. I tried to keep up with him as he went from town to town but it was just impossible. He didn't publish his itinerary; it all seemed off the cuff and whimsical. Like he was really having fun, playing with the silly sensitivities of the Pharisees and their capricious laws.

In one particular case he cautioned a man that he had cured of leprosy to keep quiet about it. Not to tell anyone, but just go and show himself to the priests so they could examine him. Despite this precaution, the man blabbed and news of Jesus continued to spread rapidly. He was once again the talk of the town. It was exciting. No one knew where he would show up next, so the sense of anticipation was electric.

When he did appear in a town, crowds generally gathered quickly. After all, his many miracles had made him a celebrity throughout the realm. So anyone with an ailment of any kind was drawn to his side, or as close to his side as it was possible to get.

Sometimes, it was truly impossible to get near him. In one instance, a group of his friends had carried a man who could not walk to the house where Jesus was, hoping that he could be cured. But by the time they arrived at the house, it was packed to the rafters. There was no way they could get through the crowd so Jesus could see their friend.

You had to be there to really grasp what happened. And fortunately, I was. There was a continual hubbub as Jesus was healing the blind, sick and lame who were brought before him. There were cheers and shouts of joy, for the crowd included not just those suffering from various ailments but also their families and friends. There was also a large contingent of curiosity seekers, eager to see this new phenomenon called Jesus of Nazareth.

And, of course there was a group of doubters, the Scribes and Pharisees who hated Jesus and felt threatened by him. They dogged his steps, always hoping to catch him in some slip up, some gaffe, some misdemeanor. They tried to be inconspicuous but were not very good at it.

It wasn't their dress that made them stand out, although they did have a unique style. It was their attitude. They were clearly not among his fans; their suspicious leers and snide comments to each other were obvious. When the crowd cheered, they grimaced; when people fell on their knees, they smirked with a superior attitude that said what are these simpletons doing?

I saw them standing in a corner of that crowded little house, whispering and winking and generally making light of the situation. Sooner or later, they had convinced themselves, Jesus would do something, anything, that they could use to bring him down. Even if it was just a minor infraction of some obscure law, they could build it into a mighty edifice of wrongdoing and use it to put him back in his place for once and for all. They were gleeful with hope that, in this huge crowd and with so much going on, surely he would do something out of line so they could pounce on him. The fact that the temperature was rising in the tiny closely packed house did not improve their mood. It was getting uncomfortably warm.

But then there came a sudden cool breeze, seemingly out of nowhere. The doors and windows had been thrown open long ago but that had not done much to reduce the overpowering heat generated by dozens of warm, smelly bodies pressed closely together. The fresh air was heavenly. People looked around, trying to find the source of the refreshing current of air. Finally, someone happened to glance upward. "Look! Look!" he shouted.

A few tiny chips of roofing tile were drifting down from the ceiling, creating little clouds of dust as they landed on the floor below. A few people started coughing as they breathed it in. In addition to the discomfort of heat and sweat, people were now inhaling dust and cobwebs falling from the rafters. But Jesus was unmoved; he knew what was happening.

But nobody else did. They craned their necks to see what was going on. What they saw caused both amazement and irritation, but also a sense of shock and fear. They saw that a small hole had been cut in the center of the roof, which was the source of the mini dust storm descending on them.

Before their eyes, the small crack in the roof began to grow, getting larger and larger as more and more dust and debris rained down upon the onlookers below. The air was getting thick and people began heading to the doors. The folks directly under the growing hole in the roof cleared away, leaving the center of the room vacant.

People grasped for an explanation. One said some animal must be up there, trying to build a nest or get in from the weather. No, another thought that it was a miracle and that God's light would soon shine in. Yet another thought it was an earthquake and the whole building was about to come down on them. The murmuring exploded to frantic screams as the crowd reacted to fear of the unknown.

Jesus merely looked up, expectantly, a slight grin on his face. The hint of his smile calmed the crowd. They had come to know Jesus, and to trust him. They finally realized that whatever was happening was not going to harm them because they were with him whom they had seen cure the ill and heal the broken. Even though this looked threatening, Jesus was there and he would make things right.

The Pharisees and Scribes had other thoughts. This was a bonanza for them, they thought, because it looked really bad for Jesus. He was clearly responsible for destroying this poor man's house, which certainly must be a big enough infraction of the law that would at least allow then to drag him before the courts and maybe put him behind bars for a time or even have him exiled. They huddled excitedly.

As if to read their thoughts the owner of the house cast a worried look at Jesus. He had trusted Jesus to let him come into his house knowing full well that a crowd of uninvited guests would soon follow. That was good, he thought, because it would enhance his popularity in the town as a righteous person who provided a base for Jesus to operate. But he never expected his home would be torn apart like this. "Who's going to fix my roof?" he shouted.

Despite all the guesswork, nobody understood what was really going on with, and on, the roof. The people stared upwards like stargazers studying the zodiac. What they saw was an ever-opening roof, the hole slowly growing inch by inch. Soon it was big enough for a small dog or cat to fall through.

Someone then shouted, "It's big enough for my ten year old kid!" Soon someone else said it was big enough for a goat, then another brought a flurry of laughter by stating even his wife could now come down from above because she always wanted to check up on him. Women looked daggers at the man. What they saw next silenced the crowd.

There were five men on the roof, and one of them was lying helpless on a mat. Four of the men looked at each other and smiled. The hole they made was now big enough for them to slowly lower their friend lying on his mat down through the roof and before the very feet of Jesus. As they cranked their homemade winch the crowd was itchy with anticipation.

"What are you doing?" someone yelled at the men on the roof.

"Well, we couldn't get in through the front door, nor the back door, nor any of the windows. Our friend needs the healing power of Jesus. He wants to walk again. We have followed Jesus from town to town and never gotten this close to him before, because we must carry this full-grown man every step of the way. But we have done it because he believes that Jesus can heal him, and because we have seen what Jesus has done. How can you blame us for doing this for our friend?"

The crowd recognized their faith and admired their creativity. They had decided that nothing would stop them in their mission to bring their friend to Jesus, even if that meant climbing on the roof and dragging him up there with them, and leaving him lying in the sun while they began to tear the roof apart. Their faith in Jesus gave them the will and the strength to do it. The man now lay before the one who called himself the Son of God. The hearts of all in the room went out to him.

Jesus looked at the man as if he had known him all his life. This whole drama: the cascading chips of roofing, the dust and straw falling down, the gaping hole in the ceiling, all of this appeared to be no surprise to him. Of course, I had long ago learned that nothing ever surprised him. But then even I was shocked by what he said next.

This man was lying on his mat, powerless. His friends had struggled to bring him to the house where Jesus was effecting cures of all sorts of ailments. Surely everyone knew why he was here.

Yet Jesus, sensing an opportunity no one else saw, said to the man: "Because of your great faith, your sins are forgiven."

The crowd let out a gasp. But the Scribes and Pharisees went wild. "This is blasphemy!" they cried, knowing that blasphemy was a major offense and this could just be the chance they were looking for. "No one has the power to forgive sins except God alone!" Once again Jesus had defied them and their false piety. Their anger surged. But Jesus saw it coming and simply said "There's no need for you to get all upset." Then he appeared to change the subject.

There was utter silence in the room when he said "Listen to me and try to understand." Then he asked, "Which is easier to say, 'your sins are forgiven', or 'get up and walk'?" The Pharisees were nonplussed. What was he talking about? But Jesus didn't wait for an answer, he raised his voice and said to the man lying at his feet, "I command you! Get up and walk! Go home to your family!" Obediently, the paralyzed man sprang to his feet, picked up his mat, flung it over his shoulder, and marched out, followed by his former bearers, filled with praise for the man who had cured their friend.

The unique circumstances of this miracle made instant news. Tongues wagged from one end of town to the other as everyone wanted to learn more about this amazing man who called himself the Son of God. The contingent of believers grew by the minute. Who could argue with the premise that only the Son of God could do such wondrous things?

Once again Jesus had shown the Scribes and Pharisees to be full of platitudes, pride and hot air. They were beginning to develop a troubling sense of powerlessness over him, for he had bested them every time they challenged him. They did not like being made to look like fools and have people laughing at them and talking about them behind their backs.

While everyone else went home that day glorifying God and singing the praises of this man named Jesus, the Scribes and Pharisees just went home. Mad. They would try again another day.

The group thinned rapidly after this miracle. As people filtered out the owner of the house again began to think of his damaged roof. Repairing it would be costly. He could hardly ask Jesus to pay for it because he had invited Jesus and his men to come to his home to boost his standing in the community. Besides, he knew his band of disciples did not have much money and, worse yet, he would have to deal with that nasty Judas to get even a shekel. But still, it wouldn't hurt to ask.

So he approached Jesus, who was about to walk out the door. "Excuse me, sir, what can we do about the roof? It's going to need to be fixed."

"Is it?" said Jesus. "What's wrong with it?"

"Don't you remember? There's a giant hole in it where some guys lowered a man down so you could cure him!"

Jesus just smiled, and pointed at the ceiling. The roof looked brand new. The owner of the house seemed surprised that his roof was already repaired, but I wasn't. If Jesus could cure the sick and lame and withered, he could certainly do minor roof repairs. He was a carpenter, after all.

A Fish Story

> Jesus said: "Don't be afraid. From now on you will catch men." And, bringing their boats to shore, they left everything and followed him. Luke 5.10

I WAS WALKING ALONG the shore of Lake Genesareth one morning. It was a beautiful day and I had set out on a little stroll to enjoy the day and get some fresh air. As I ambled along I noticed a good-sized group of people up ahead. It's a nice day, I thought, maybe they also decided to get out and enjoy it.

As I came nearer, however, I saw that it was not a group of picnickers or sightseers. It was disciplined and structured, more like a class or lecture, and one man was doing all the talking. It was Jesus, of course. And the crowd was listening intently. I tried to get up close enough so I could hear what he was saying, but the group kept growing as more and more people became aware of what was going on. His popularity was such that all he had to do was strike up a conversation with a few people and eventually he was surrounded by a crowd.

Besides the folks standing on the shore, there were several boats on the water. I recognized Simon, one of the fishers of men that Jesus had gathered about him. He was repairing his nets and did not look very happy. I was confused at that, since he must have been glad to see Jesus and get a chance to hear him.

Jesus finally called out to him, and Simon asked what he wanted him to do. By this time the group surrounding Jesus had grown so large that they crowded in on him, causing him to keep backing up to avoid being crushed. Then I realized why he had called to Simon. Just a few more steps backward retreating from his listeners and he would have fallen into the lake.

So he got into the boat and Simon rowed just a little off the shore. Far enough out that Jesus was safe from the pressing bodies yet close enough so he could sit down in the boat and continue talking. I was surprised that his voice carried so well that the audience could still hear him clearly. The boat was only ten or fifteen feet out but that was enough to give him the room he needed. It was a floating lectern.

Some of the listeners sat down on the sand, which still felt cool this early in the day. Others remained standing. There were a few children running around playing tag, unaware of who Jesus was and why all these people were gathered there. One was making a temple out of sand and a number of his friends were giving him advice on what it should look like. They argued briefly about who should play the role of the High Priest when the temple was done, but one of the parents shussed them and they quieted down.

Meanwhile Jesus was telling his audience about his mission and inviting them to turn their eyes to the Lord and repent of their sins. They had heard some of this before. Many recalled John, who had baptized Jesus in the Jordan. He was an impressive prophet and dynamic speaker, but Jesus was different. He instructed them with authority and answered questions with a level of confidence that they found both comforting and challenging.

The Pharisees, as usual, stood off to one side in their own little group, sneering and laughing at the foolish people who came here to listen to this rustic itinerant preacher. And what was his message? A joke, and worse than that. He was talking blasphemy. Undoing the laws that dictated the daily lives of the people and calling himself the Son of God? They were angered at the size of the crowds he drew and the devotion of his gang of men-fishers.

They would like to write him off as just another flash-in-the-pan quasi holy man but they had to admit he seemed to be much more than that. They had been unable to trip him up or beat him in an argument, though they had tried many times. But this scene with him preaching from a boat they found just too silly and childish for words.

They watched with disdain and a growing bitterness as Jesus calmly answered even the most difficult questions put to him and offered wise advice to help people solve their problems. They could get nothing past him; he anticipated their every move. Finally, seeing that Jesus had finished speaking and the crowd was drifting off, they expressed their frustration by kicking down the children's little temple of sand.

But Jesus was not yet through. He saw the disappointed look on Simon's face and knew the reason for it. "Let's go fishing," he said, with an encouraging smile. But Simon just shook his head and said that he and his crew had been out all night without catching so much as a sardine. "I don't think there are any fish in this lake," he told Jesus. "I'm not sure that fish even exist!"

Jesus knew that Simon was a man of extremes, given to loud outbursts that he later regretted, but also prone to fierce bouts of despair and grief. With Simon, everything was black or white, wonderful or terrible, friend or foe. There was no middle ground with this man. But that was what Jesus liked about him, why he had chosen him. He was just the firebrand he needed to lead his movement.

Jesus locked eyes with Simon. A gentle power emanated from him. It was as if he looked right through him. Simon, gruff and grizzled, melted. He shrugged his huge shoulders and motioned his crew to get ready to cast off.

One could imagine that Simon certainly knew more about fishing than Jesus did. After all, it was his life and livelihood. But what I saw as I waited on that shore told a different story. I was the only person still there; everyone else had gone home, even the Pharisees.

Peter and his crew got on board and took off, with Jesus controlling the tiller. The boat grew smaller and smaller as it sailed farther off toward the horizon. I was waiting to see how far out they were going before casting the nets. I think I could hear some of what they were saying. Voices travel so well over the water. It seemed Simon found several spots he thought might hold a fish or two but Jesus kept shaking his head and the boat kept getting smaller and smaller. They were just about out of sight when the commotion began.

A huge shout went up from the crew. Did someone fall overboard? No problem, I thought, Jesus could rescue him. By now I believed he could do anything. The shouting continued and even grew in intensity. Soon I saw another boat approaching Simon's, so far out that I could barely see it. I had no idea what was going on. I was convinced that some catastrophe had taken place, that someone was injured or had drowned.

But then the yelling I heard over the water started to sound a lot like laughter. Like they were having a party out there in the middle of the lake. I couldn't believe it. I had experienced many weird goings on since I had come to know Jesus but this was the strangest yet. I waited with anticipation as I saw the boats turning around and heading to shore.

But I could barely see the boats. It was as if the men were floating right on the water itself. The boats must have been leaking because they were barely staying afloat. A few of the men were swimming alongside the boats, I guess to take some of the weight out of the crafts. When they finally got close enough I could see what was really happening.

I never saw so many fish! Both boats were filled to overflowing with fresh, beautiful, lively fish. Hundreds of them, no thousands. More than I could count. Needless to say, Simon and his men were overjoyed. A few had tears running down their cheeks because they were laughing so hard. Simon was all smiles. Jesus just looked at him, knowingly, as if to say: See, Simon, fish do exist.

There was so much joking and laughing and good cheer among Jesus and his friends that I don't think they even saw me. But I believe Jesus did. As he turned to look back to where I was standing, he noticed the temple of sand that the Pharisees had destroyed, and with just a quick glance, rebuilt it.

The Twelve

> He called to himself those he wanted, and they came to him. He picked twelve so he could send them out to preach. He gave them the power to cure infirmities and cast out demons. Mark 3.13

As Jesus was traveling in and around the local towns and villages there was always a contingent of hangers-on following him. The groupies usually included a few of his favorite apostles: Simon, of course, who could forget him? And a tax collector named Matthew. Then there was John, just a lad, but nevertheless a full-fledged member of the group.

I knew a few of his followers personally, and I myself had often dreamt that one day he might choose me to join him. But, despite my best efforts, I had never even spoken to the man, and so I realized I had little chance of making the team. But a few of my friends seemed to be in the running to help him in his work, and, I must confess, I was still hopeful too.

I had more than just a passing interest in Jesus at this point. Having been aware of him from practically the very moment of his birth, and having followed him since then whenever I could, I found myself inextricably drawn to him. I felt I knew him, in a sense, and I liked him.

He did everything right. Always said the right thing, always knew the answer in every circumstance. He did everything with a style that seemed smooth and effortless, almost godlike. He was a walking miracle and I wanted desperately to meet him. He had called himself the Son of God on many occasions and, given the way he carried himself and the good works he performed, he could be what, or who, he says he is.

Everybody already knew that Simon was the top man in his group; and that James and John and a few others were already on the team. But, it seemed to me, if Jesus really wanted to create a mass movement he needed a lot more people involved.

And so it was that, when I heard the rumors that Jesus was going to be taking a look at possible recruits, I hastened to join the group of wannabe disciples. They had gathered at the base of a mountain after having heard that Jesus had spent the night on that very mountain, probably thinking things over and setting the standards of behavior and personality for the men he would be choosing. After all, he needed the best if his plan were to succeed.

I had no idea how many people he would be selecting, and it seems, neither did anyone else, for there were several hundred men, and a few women, who showed up. I could not fathom how all these people heard of this contest, but word must have spread quickly. In fact, people were still queuing up, some even bringing their families along. It was a quiet crowd, but filled with intensity as folks sensed the seriousness of the occasion.

When Jesus came down from the mountain he was all business. He called Simon and James and John and a few others over to him and they surrounded him almost like a palace guard. He surprised everyone by declaring that Simon would henceforth be known as Peter, which he explained meant Rock. That made sense to me. This man was a Rock in every sense of the word: Brash and bold, loud, daring and brave. A good choice for a leader, and good choice of a name.

I remembered a couple others who had been with Jesus since the beginning of his career: I knew Andrew, the brother of Simon

Peter; and Matthew, the tax collector. However, I found it odd that someone in that profession could be part of Jesus' team. I don't think there was a tax collector in the entire country, if not the world, who wasn't a crook. If Matthew was actually honest in his dealings with tax-paying citizens then he was truly a special guy and Jesus had made a good choice.

In fact, Jesus hadn't given Matthew much of a chance to say no to his invitation to join him. He simply marched into his counting house one afternoon, unannounced and unexpected, and said "Follow me." It was that simple.

Matthew, sensing an opportunity to put real meaning into his life by becoming a follower of Jesus instead of just a toady for the Romans, left his lucrative business right then and there. He told his assistants to take over and said he wasn't sure when or if he'd be back. A real decision maker, that Matthew! I liked him immediately. If he stayed on as a disciple he'd be giving up the chance for a lot of illegal loot.

Now things got confusing. Jesus picked another guy named James. He already had selected James the son of Zebedee, and the brother of John, while they were out fishing. This new James would be called the "Less," I guess because the other James got picked first.

Then Jesus added further complications by naming another Simon to the team. But, since he had already changed the first Simon's name to Peter the Rock, I guess we really still had only one Simon. This new Simon was part of a radical band called the Zealots, a rebellious group that was avidly working to overthrow the Romans. He would henceforth be known as Simon the Zealot. I was happy to see him chosen as he seemed to be a pretty tough, fearless character. But I was interested to see how he would get along with Matthew, who was virtually on the payroll of the Roman establishment Simon was fighting against.

I was not very impressed with the next man Jesus picked. His name was Thomas. He was a twin, but that wasn't what bothered me about him. He just seemed very unsure of himself, very doubtful, as if he didn't know for certain exactly why he was here and why he had been selected. Sometimes twins are like that. They're so used to being part of a team that they often lack self esteem and find it hard to think for themselves as unique individuals. But he seemed eager and I hoped he might grow into the job.

I was getting concerned by this time because Jesus had not even looked in my direction even once. I didn't want to create a scene by pointing out who I was and how I had followed him all these years. I felt I was qualified and would have liked to get some sort of recognition, so that even if I wasn't chosen as a full-fledged disciple I could at least get a consolation prize. But no, his gaze never came my way.

The next few choices were newcomers to me. Two guys named Philip and Bartholomew were added to the list. But now I was confused once again, for Bartholomew was also known as Nathaniel. We already had two Apostles with the same name: James; now we have one with two names! Jesus had met both of them previously and evidently thought they would be worthy to serve in his mission.

OK, so now we had, for sure: Simon Peter and his brother Andrew; James and John, the sons of Zebedee; Philip and Bartholomew (Nathaniel); James the Less and Simon the Zealot; Matthew the tax man; and lastly, Thomas. Ten, a nice round number, but hardly a big enough group to effectively spread the word of the great accomplishments and promise Jesus had to offer to the world. I think he needed more men, a lot more.

And I was ready. I was awaiting his call when he just looked the other way and picked a pretty sad-looking character named Jude. I had never heard of him and I was not impressed. I would have been a better pick, for sure. Then Jesus threw us another curve, for this Jude was also called Thaddeus. Now it seemed half of the group had at least two names and maybe even three.

Now we had eleven, and I thought perhaps an even dozen would be a good number. Again I was hoping to catch Jesus' eye but he didn't even glance in my direction. Instead he called on another guy named Jude! That made two Simons, two Jameses, and two Judes. Any gatherings with this team would have to be very confusing. If Jesus said "Hey Jude," these two guys would come running.

If I thought the first Jude was a questionable choice, I really didn't like the second one. He had a sleazy, shifty-eyed look about him, as if he had some deep, dark secret to hide. This Jude was an odd one all right, but if Jesus had chosen him he must have some purpose, some role to play in this whole story. I think I would have been a better choice.

His name was really Judas. Jesus made him general manager for the group, responsible for finances as well as keeping the team fed and clothed and housed. He would be in a very tempting position, holding the power of the purse, small as it was for so fledgling an organization.

I thought it might have been better if Jesus had chosen Matthew to handle the money matters for his outfit. He had professional financial experience, which would have been very helpful for a start-up group like this that was just scraping by. Maybe he was tainted in Jesus' mind by the general reputation of tax collectors as cheats and embezzlers, even though he wasn't guilty of any of that. Anyway, Judas got the job and I'm sure Jesus had his reasons for trusting him.

So that was it. Jesus called an end to the meeting and sent us all home. There was some grumbling, but I have to say that, in a sense, I was relieved not to have been called. I would have had to give up so much: my comfortable home and position in life, my family and friends and evenings at the tavern.

I expected that a lot of travel would be involved for Jesus and his crew, for they were venturing into completely unknown territory and against tremendous odds and potential for danger, not the least of which might come from Jesus' own people.

I had noticed the scowling and sneers of the Scribes and Pharisees as they watched from a distance.

An Afternoon on the Mount

> Going down with them he stood in a level spot. There was a group of his disciples and a large crowd of people ... who had come to hear him and be cured of their illnesses. Luke 6. 17,18

JESUS, EVEN THOUGH he must have known that the Pharisees were out to get him, didn't change his tune in an attempt to improve relations with them. I was a little perplexed by this because, after all, they were the recognized leaders in the community. People kowtowed to them and gave them great respect, regardless of whether they earned it or not.

They were pompous, arrogant and bossy, ever on the lookout for infractions of the law, of which they were the sole judges and jury. Most people stayed out of their way and made every attempt not to cross them lest they incur their wrath. I thought it would have been a practical move for Jesus to work out some kind of compromise with them, but he clearly wasn't interested in playing their game.

In fact, rather than bow to these petty demigods, Jesus seemed to go out of his way to challenge them every chance he got. They remembered the incident in the temple with great bitterness. It seemed that after that event they had declared open war against this man who called himself the Son of God, a claim they found to be ridiculous.

But Jesus had something special in store for them on a very nice day as he was preaching on the side of a grassy knoll. Not a mountain, but a nice gentle hill that provided a slightly elevated platform from which he could see the people below and speak to them. A better location and opportunity for a lecture could hardly be imagined.

And lecture he did. This was the first time that I could remember when Jesus laid out his ideas of what he thought life was really all about. He was mesmerizing as he related his principles for happiness and a righteous life. However, his thoughts were quite the opposite of what people had been hearing from their unelected leaders, the Scribes and Pharisees.

He spoke in very simple, short sentences, yet his words became more and more potent as they sank into the hearts and minds of his listeners. Like aphorisms, they were brief, yet filled with deep meaning. I soon realized that Jesus was not just giving us his opinion on things, he was laying out a master plan for a complete transformation of our thinking and way of acting toward each other. In particular he was challenging the mindset that the Scribes and Pharisees had dictated for the people. This is what he said:

"It is not the rich and powerful who will obtain eternal life, but those who are often shunned and ignored by the world. They are laughed at by the world but they are blessed by my Father."

Then he continued,

"Those who are poor in spirit are blessed, for theirs is the kingdom of heaven.

"It will be the meek who shall inherit the earth.

"Those who mourn will be comforted.

"If you seek after justice you will be satisfied.

"Be merciful to others and you will receive mercy.

"The clean of heart shall see God.

"Peacemakers are the children of God.

"If you suffer for seeking justice you will inherit the kingdom of heaven.

"Especially blessed are you when you are reviled and persecuted for my sake. Rejoice, for your reward will be great in heaven."

His words fell like little bombs, simple and straightforward, yet complex. Jesus knew what he was saying was upsetting the Pharisees. He was purposely turning their world upside down and rewriting the rules that traditionally define success in the eyes of the world.

When he said that humble and lowly people are blessed by God, and not those who exalt themselves, I saw some of the Pharisees wince as if stabbed by a tiny dagger. They were convinced that they, not low-class rubes such as these Jesus-followers, were the ones who deserved the Kingdom of Heaven. It was self-evident to them, for they were convinced their positions of power were well-deserved.

Likewise, when he said that those who were gentle and loving and giving would inherit the earth, they smirked at him and at the people on the side of the mount, who were beginning to nod their heads in appreciation and understanding. They liked the idea of a potential reward for leading a righteous life.

When Jesus elevated mourning to a virtue, identifying it as a special opportunity for divine consolation, it flew directly in the face of the Scribes and Pharisees. In their minds, sorrow and adversity and mourning were not signs of heavenly favor; they were miseries justly imposed by God on those who sinned and failed to follow the law. They were now beginning to regard him with open hostility.

But he was just getting started. He announced that the pursuit of justice was a virtue, and that people who seek it night and day will ultimately benefit from its intervention in their lives. To the Pharisees that was outrageous! Justice is not something that the rabble can obtain like picking fruit off a tree. Justice is meted out by the courts, which are controlled by the elite, by the very people he was insulting so arrogantly.

Celebrating the practice of mercy flabbergasted the Pharisees. They had no use for it. Even the very concept of mercy was unheard of in their overly legalistic minds. The law dealt with real, concrete facts. Did Nathan slaughter a goat on the Sabbath or not? If he did, he's guilty. There's no excuse for not observing the law even in its most intricate details; and they would judge violators strictly on facts, showing no mercy.

I think some of them wanted to walk away at this point. They had heard enough. It was as if every word Jesus spoke was directed right at them. The other listeners were enjoying themselves, however, mainly because what Jesus was saying was what they wanted to hear, and also because they saw the obvious discomfort he was causing the members of this elite and hated caste.

But they stayed on and listened, and were probably sorry that they did. They were confused when he said that those who were pure and clean of heart would see God. "See God?" The Pharisees considered themselves to be perfectly clean of heart, yet they had not seen God, so how could these illiterate fools who were so taken by his words be allowed to do so?

He said that those who sought after peace and tranquility among men would become so beloved by God as to be called his own children. I doubt that any of the Scribes or Pharisees in attendance ever gave a second thought to the concept of peace, being constantly engaged in an almost warlike struggle for power and influence.

Jesus then rocked their world even further by saying that there was a special place in heaven for those who suffered persecution for the sake of justice. Furthermore, he added that those the world mocks and reviles are truly blessed, especially if they are persecuted because they believe in him. Revel in it, he said, because you will receive a great reward in heaven for being faithful to me.

This was all too much for them. I overheard a few of the Pharisees grumbling among themselves. Their overall attitude was one of unbelief. Not only did they not believe in him and who he said he was; they could not believe that he was putting forth such radical ideas.

"Blessed are the meek? I don't get it," said one. "Poor in spirit? What does that even mean?" said another. "Clean of heart? Well, he must mean us," said another. And thus they went on: each thought carefully parsed and questioned. Merciful obtaining mercy? Peacemakers as children of God? Clean of heart seeing God? And worst of all, a reward in heaven for being persecuted on earth? Their judgment: He was preaching utter nonsense!

In a matter of fifteen or twenty minutes Jesus had erased one concept of the world and replaced it with another. He said that, regardless of what some people thought, those lowest in the world's opinion: the humble, the needy, the striving, the hopeless and helpless and miserable, the poor and downtrodden and persecuted and despairing; they were the ones on whom God's favor rested. Not the proud and mighty and precocious, the rulers and arbiters of the people, the lawgivers and law enforcers. God's face did not shine on them. They have their reward here on earth, while the meek and humble will find a great reward awaiting them in heaven.

They began to feel their elevated status crumbling right beneath their feet. But Jesus was not through yet. He had a few more surprises for them.

Jesus Rewrites the Rules

> "And all who hear my words and do not follow them, will be like a fool who builds his house on sand."
> Matthew 7.26

AFTER SETTING THOSE basic principles of life, Jesus proceeded to dictate some new rules of behavior, further distancing himself from the Old Law. The ways of the Scribes and Pharisees were no longer sufficient for salvation, he maintained. It was necessary to go beyond the law, to be more just, more holy, more humble. I carefully wrote down what he was saying in my diary so I could remember it and share it with others.

The Old Law, Jesus explained, forbids taking another's life. I thought everyone would agree it is a sin to kill another person. "This is not about murder," he said. "I tell you, even if you just have hatred in your heart for another, you are guilty of sin. Do not come to offer sacrifice to God if you have bitterness in your heart for your fellow man." It was becoming clear to me that, according to Jesus, God wanted more than just simple observance of the letter of the law.

Likewise, he continued, the Old Law did not adequately communicate the principles of a virtuous relationship between man and wife. No one would disagree that adultery is certainly a sin. But Jesus said "I tell you if you even just look at a woman with lewd thoughts, you have already committed adultery with her in your heart." Avoid temptation no matter the cost, he said, even if it means the loss of a limb or one of the senses. Again Jesus was going beyond what the law said, to the very spirit behind it.

Then he surprised everyone by revising the *lex talionis*, the Old Law of Talion, which demanded extreme and exact justice: An eye for an eye and a tooth for a tooth. Jesus advocated a totally different reaction to violence and mayhem. Instead of fighting to exact revenge, he urged peaceful accommodation. If someone strikes you, "turn the other cheek," he said. The Pharisees scoffed loudly.

Jesus reaffirmed that we must love our neighbor. But, he said "It is equally important that you love your enemy. Love those who hate you. For if you just love your friends, you are no better than the Pharisees." They were notorious for secret gatherings and exclusive cliques with their friends, while loathing everyone else.

"And, when you pray or give alms," he said, "don't let the whole world know about it. You will receive a greater reward if your prayer is between you and God. When you give to the poor and needy, do not let your piety become a subject of discussion in the town. Let there be no competition to see who can appear to be the holiest and most prayerful and generous." I began to feel a little guilty, as some of what he was saying started to sound like he was talking about me.

Likewise, I blushed when he said "If you are fasting don't walk around with a long face so everyone can see how pitiful and penitential you are. Dress up in your finest and have a smile on your face. Your father in heaven will appreciate what you are doing in secret and smile upon you in return. By behaving this way you are storing up great treasures in heaven."

Jesus was certainly painting a different picture of piety and righteousness from what we were accustomed to. But, he made sense, at least to me. He was advocating a personal response to God, rather than one that simply fulfilled the strictures of the law.

Sure, we must obey the law, but we must go beyond it if we want to achieve true holiness.

He said we must trust in God, and not worry about what we're going to eat or wear or where we will live. He said we should observe how well the Lord cares for his creatures, the birds and plants around us. "Are the lilies not beautiful?" he asked with a smile. "And the birds, don't they have plenty to eat? If God takes such good care of these won't he be so much more concerned for your welfare and happiness?" I think what Jesus meant was that worrying too much about worldly things like clothes and food and houses will mean neglecting the things that really count: God and heaven and the quest for eternal life.

Jesus reminded us of the power of prayer. He said we should not fear to ask God for what we need. He compared our concern for our children's needs and wants and how we desire to take good care of them, to how God looks upon us as his children. I think he was suggesting that we should be more like little children approaching God in prayer as a child approaches its mom or dad for something good to eat.

Jesus ended his soliloquy by telling his listeners that his comments were not just idle ramblings. He was serious. These were rules to live by. He gave us an example to anchor that thought in our minds. He said "consider the man who wishes to build a new home for himself and his family. If he is wise, he will survey the surrounding area and set his foundation firmly on rock. His home will be sturdy and long-lasting, able to withstand the harsh pounding of storms and wind. This is the man who pays attention to what I am saying and acts on my principles."

Then he continued, "On the other hand, there are some who will ignore my message. He might as well be building his house on sand. When the storms come there is nothing he can do but watch it being blown away. He will run to his wise neighbor, who heeded my words and built his home on rock."

Rock. I immediately thought of Peter, and wondered if Jesus, in fact, was also building something, maybe not an edifice, but something invisible and spiritual, on a different kind of rock. But a rock nonetheless.

How to Pray

> "And I tell you, ask and you will get what you want; seek and you will find what you are looking for; knock and doors will open for you." Luke 11.9

AFTER JESUS FINISHED speaking to the crowd on that little hillock, most people started drifting away. However, a couple of people came up to him and asked, "When we pray, what should we say to God? What words should we use?"

Jesus responded with a most beautiful but brief prayer that encompassed a multitude of realities about God and man. I tried to write down what he was saying as he spoke, but I'm afraid I really only got the main points. Ever since I began following Jesus around I always had scraps of papyrus with me to take notes on his doings and sayings, so at least I had an outline.

"Our Father," was how he began. And I remembered that just those two words were enough to cause a stir in the crowd. We were not accustomed to calling God "Father." He was generally called Creator, Ruler, or, most fearfully, Judge. He was often angry, and with good cause, as people frequently ignored his mandates. He had punished mankind with floods and plagues. To call him Father was to remove all that fierce anger and re-imagine God as no longer a Judge, but an Advocate, a Helper.

Jesus himself had suggested that very idea in his parable about the father who had two sons, one of whom squandered his fortune in "loose living," and came back home crying and destitute.

Whereupon his father greeted the returning prodigal with a big feast, at which he did even more crying than his son. I think a father would have a hard time being a judge.

Jesus had often spoken of God as "His" Father, but now he was saying that he was also ours. To say that God was "Our" Father implied a personal relationship that was unheard of among his listeners. It implied a level of intimacy that opened the door to direct communication with the Almighty. If God is Our Father, we can now approach him as his children, confident that he will listen to our needs.

If Jesus would have stopped right there he would have given me enough to think about for a hundred years!

In fact, I was so busy contemplating the ramifications of God being my Father that I barely remembered the rest of what he had to say. But I do recall the main points:

He said Our Father dwells in heaven, and is exalted and far above us in all ways.

He said his name was sacred and must be treated respectfully.

He said we should try to make God's kingdom a reality on earth, and make his will known here just as it is in heaven.

Our Father will provide us with the Bread of Life every day, just as he gave manna to the Israelites in the desert.

We must forgive others if we expect Our Father to forgive our sins.

He said we should seek Our Father's help to avoid temptation, as we are too weak to fight it by ourselves.

Finally, he said we should ask Our Father to protect us from Satan, who is real and is among us right now, searching for those whose faith is weak so he can use them for his diabolical plans.

With this awesome prayer Jesus covered a lot of territory in just a few words, but for me, his main message was a simple one: God is Our Father. My Father; and yours.

Jesus called himself the Son of God. I think in this prayer he is telling me that I can call myself a son of God also. I can then logically say Jesus is my brother, and maybe my friend. I saw this as a tremendous honor; and I must add, a tremendous responsibility.

Reaching Out To Rome

> "For I too am subject to authority, and have men under me. I say to one, 'Go', and he goes, and to another 'Come', and he comes. And when I tell my servant to do something he does it." Matthew 8.9

WHILE PONDERING THE new standards of behavior that Jesus was advocating, or, I should say, demanding of us, I was struck with a sudden awareness of the authority and conviction with which he spoke. He was not merely asking us to change our ways; he was basically telling us this is the way it's going to be in his world. And I believe he really was talking about an entirely new world, where people would act differently toward each other. It was a calmer, more peaceful world, and I liked the thought of it. I think I was coming to believe in Jesus and what he promised.

My faith was further solidified a little later when word got around of a couple of his most recent exploits. By this time practically anything he did immediately became big news in the community. Rumors and speculation abounded. As much as he cautioned people not to talk about the things he did, the gossipmongers would not be silenced.

For instance, when he restored hearing and clear speech to a deaf man at the Decapolis Jesus told the onlookers to keep quiet about it. But it made no difference, in fact, it just made him that much more of a phenomenon in their sight. There was always a sense of expectation about him, a sense of wonder. He was an instant topic of conversation, despite his efforts to stay out of the limelight.

At Capharnaum, Jesus was approached by a very anguished centurion whose servant was suffering from paralysis and in terrible pain. Jesus asked if the man wanted him to come and see his servant so he could cure him, but the centurion demurred with the words: "I am not worthy to have you come into my house. I believe you can cure him with just a word, here and now, without making the trip to my home."

Jesus seemed surprised at the man's faith. He was a Roman, and accordingly should have looked down upon a Hebrew as a member of a lower and despised class of people. But now he was saying that he, the proud Roman, was the one who was not worthy and Jesus was to be treated with honor. The man explained. "I have many men under me. They do whatever I tell them. I control their comings and goings, so I understand authority and power. And I see it in you, and I respect it."

Jesus said "Look at this man's faith. A Roman. He has stronger faith that any Israelite I have met so far. The kingdom of God is big enough for the people of all the world, not just the followers of Abraham, Isaac and Jacob." Then he said to the centurion, "Be on your way. Your servant is waiting for you." I later learned that his servant was cured at that very moment.

I was amazed at this story. Not because Jesus had worked a miracle remotely without even going to see the centurion's servant, but because of his reaction to the man's faith. Many of us were of the opinion that Jesus' main task was to rebuild the nation of Israel, but here he was praising a Roman and even suggesting that the faith he was offering was meant not just for the people of Israel, but also for Rome and for the entire world.

At the same time I found it odd that a Roman, a pagan, would treat Jesus with such respect, while some of his own people, particularly the Scribes and Pharisees, looked down on him and even tried to frustrate him at every opportunity.

This man embraced the power and authority of Jesus more readily than the educated elites who made up the leadership of Israel. The thought made me cringe a bit, because I could see how it could lead to some terrible consequences.

I think one of his little stories, he called them "parables," might explain his comment about the centurion's faith. In this particular parable, Jesus said faith is like a seed that a farmer plants in the ground. All the seeds come out of a large sack and are all identical. "How then," he asked, "can you explain that, when the seeds germinate and grow into mature plants, some are more healthy and productive than others. What causes this variation?" Knowing Jesus had the answer we just listened.

He said that the different outcomes are due to the type of soil that welcomes the seed from the sower's hand. "If the seed lands on rock the birds will just come down and eat it up. On extremely dry soil it won't have enough water and the sun will scorch it. But if it lands on fertile moist loamy ground it will grow and yield a great harvest for the farmer."

I think in this parable Jesus was saying that we are the soil. He was the sower, and the seed was the promise he was offering us. He was offering us a valuable gift, each of us hearing the same message. Some welcomed it with reservation and doubt, others with extreme gratitude and thankfulness. Some, the Scribes and Pharisees, looked on it with complete scorn. We all had heard his message of promise and hope; and the centurion had embraced it most firmly. He was good soil for the seed Jesus was planting.

Calming the Tempest

> And when it was getting late in the day, he said "Let's go to the other side." And dismissing the crowd, they took him as he was into the boat. Mark 4.35

LATER THAT DAY he told his disciples that he wanted to get away from the crowds for awhile and would like to sail to the opposite shore of the lake. It was getting late but the water seemed calm and there was just a gentle breeze. It would require some rowing but they should make good time and get there before dark.

So they gathered in the boat, Jesus among them, and cast off. He had had a long day, with many interactions with the maimed and ailing. It was exhausting. He could feel power going out from him, even when a woman suffering from a hemorrhage had just touched his cloak.

Not surprisingly, he fell asleep before they had even gone halfway. He needed the rest, his crew said to themselves. "I don't know how he does it, day after day after day." They never knew there were so many crippled and deaf people, and lepers too. Yet Jesus was always willing to listen to them and to cure their ailments, always admonishing them that their faith was what was responsible for their cure. No wonder he was tired.

It was about that time, with the darkness closing in on them, that the breeze began to sharpen, and the waves began to swell. No problem, they thought, we're within sight of the opposite shore. This will blow over.

But then a sudden blast of wind burst upon them, rocking the boat and knocking two of the men to the deck. The waves were boiling, and even began to come over the sides. Water was pooling at the bottom of the boat. Now it began to rain and quickly turned into a downpour. Even though the storm grew more violent, Jesus was still sound asleep. Should they wake him? Why? What could he do, even if he were awake?

They still had not gotten the message. Their faith in him was still in its infancy. They still did not truly believe who he was. Good thing Jesus was asleep, because he'd be disappointed at their weak faith. Were they such poor soil for the seed of his faith?

Finally their fear overcame them and they rushed to Jesus to wake him up. "We're going under," they shouted. He shook himself awake and looked at them with placid eyes, as if to say, "What's the problem? What's the big crisis?" He calmly looked about and saw the waves breaching the sides of the boat and heard the roaring of the wind and felt the sting of the pelting rain.

"We're going to drown! Don't you care?" they cried. Jesus yawned, slowly stood up in the rocking boat and looked at them. Then, raising his voice, he commanded "Stop!" And the wind immediately abated. Then he said, again in a loud voice: "Be still!" And the water was soon smooth as glass. All was peaceful, quiet and calm. Shaking his head, he looked at them questioningly.

"Why are you so afraid? What has happened to your faith?" He was not angry, but you could tell he was convinced he still had a lot of work to do with this bunch. They had all the right intentions. He had chosen them wisely and they were perfect for the jobs he had in mind for them. But they didn't know it yet. They still needed to be coddled.

If he was going to compare them in this story about the sower and his seed he would have to say that they were still tender little seedlings, apt to be uprooted if a crisis developed, still unable to face serious adversity, and still not sure who he really was.

For their part, I later heard from one of them that they had no doubt that he had special gifts, but not sure how special they were and totally unsure what plans he had in store for them. But they made it to shore, happy to be on dry land again, and asking themselves: "Who is this man who cures the sick and the blind and lame, and even the wind and seas obey him?"

A Surprise Picnic

> Jesus said to them: "There is no need to for them to go; you yourselves can give them something to eat."
> Matthew 14.16

TO GET AWAY from the pressure of the crowds that were constantly following him, Jesus asked his disciples to accompany him to a remote place called Bethsaida. It was a small community, and Jesus hoped he could sneak away without the crowds knowing that he was going there. But they got word of his journey and gathered, as usual, to see and hear him. Not wanting to miss this opportunity to see Jesus, I was there also.

Although he must have been exhausted, Jesus rose to the occasion and spoke to the people. He cured their illnesses and ailments, and urged them to atone for their sins. He reiterated his standards for a virtuous life, especially stressing the importance of love of neighbor as oneself. They listened rapt with attention.

While Jesus was talking, I noticed some tense looks among his disciples. Peter was waving his arms around and pointing at the crowd. A couple of the other guys were looking around as well. What's going on, I asked myself and tried to inch my way closer so I could hear what was happening. I snaked through the crowd slowly, raising a few unfriendly comments as I did so.

It was about that time that I realized how late it was and, consequently, that I was hungry. I had lost track of time. We were in a remote place and had been there for most of the day. Some people had brought a little food with them but most had not, and whatever little they did have was now surely gone. I suppose they thought they would be home by now, but the power of Jesus' words kept them glued to the spot. These folks were weak from hunger, and could not just be sent on their way.

But, I thought, where would you find enough food for so many hungry mouths? I guessed there must have been about five thousand men there, plus many women and even a few children. Finally I got close enough to hear what the disciples were saying.

I quickly learned that was exactly what the fuss was about. The disciples were at their wit's end trying to figure out what to do. I guess they were hungry too. "We can't send them home," said one. "They'd never make it on their empty stomachs," said another.

For all his bravado and bluster, even Peter did not have the answer. But he thought he knew who did. "Let's ask the Lord," he said. And so they did. Peter, with all the confidence of his leadership position, strode up to Jesus and explained the situation.

Jesus simply said: "Tell the people to sit down and be comfortable." Nonplussed, the disciples shook their heads and looked at each other. What is he thinking? But, reading their thoughts, Jesus added: "Tell them we're going to give them something to eat."

Their hands went up in alarm as they heard his words. "Impossible!" was the first word I heard. "There are no shops nearby where we can buy anything." Judas checked his purse and interjected that there wasn't enough money on hand to buy so great a quantity of food even if it were available. In desperation, Peter asked Jesus: "Where are we going to get enough food to satisfy this mob?" "Who is going to feed them?"

"You are," Jesus said.

It was at this point that one of the disciples, Andrew, I believe, noticed a young lad with a picnic basket standing nearby. The boy opened it when Andrew approached him, and it proved to contain five barley loaves and a couple of fish within. Andrew looked at Jesus with a mixture of delight and confusion.

Jesus said: "Bring it here." Andrew lifted the basket from the boy's arms and presented it to Jesus, who immediately looked inside. "This will do," he said. By this time most of the people were ready for a picnic, having found comfortable positions throughout the vast area. Their faces revealed a gamut of emotions and expectations.

I shared these confused reactions, but then I realized this was exactly the kind of situation Jesus was always talking about. Rational thought was insufficient to handle this reality. What was needed was faith. Now I knew what Jesus was thinking and how he was using this situation to once again show his disciples that they must not waver in their faith. I bet he was tired of having to do this over and over again.

After examining the bread and fish Jesus said "These look good enough to eat." He then blessed them and started handing them out to the disciples for distribution to the hungry horde. Each of the disciples picked up a basket and began serving the bread and fish.

As they worked their way through the crowd, they were amazed that their baskets never became empty. They were bottomless! Smiling faces greeted them everywhere, for the food was good, very good, and there was plenty of it.

Because all twelve of the disciples, plus a few extra helpers, were involved, the distribution of the picnic lunch was carried out quickly and efficiently. After everyone was through eating, they were able to refill each of the twelve baskets with the leftovers. As it was still light enough, most began their trip home, well fortified for the journey. I lingered about, however, hoping to catch Jesus' eye and maybe have a word with him. But it was impossible to get near him. I would have to try another time.

I did overhear a few of his men talking about their experience. Peter, of course, was bragging, giving the impression that he knew all along what Jesus would do. His faith was never in question, but the rest of them were lacking in the dedication and devotion to Jesus that only he possessed. As their leader, he rebuked them and urged them to try to follow his example better next time.

As I was walking away, I saw Jesus observing Peter's lecture. He just shook his head, and the slightest smile crossed his lips. He had another surprise in store for him.

Walking On the Water

> Jesus ordered the disciples to get into the boat and precede him across the sea while he sent the crowd away. Then he went to the mountainside to pray. It was now evening and he was alone. Matthew 14.22

AS THE WELL-FED picnickers were heading back to their homes, some of them began talking about what they had just heard and the miraculous food they had eaten. Perhaps because they had been weak with hunger, they had failed to grasp the full magnitude of what Jesus had done.

By feeding a crowd of better than five thousand with just a couple fish and a few loaves of bread he had defied the rules of both nutrition and arithmetic. Now, however, having had time to reflect, they were overwhelmed in their excitement about this man and the extraordinary performance they had just witnessed.

They were becoming convinced that this Jesus was no ordinary man. Nobody had ever done the kind of things he did or acted as he did. Never before had there been a man who brought about so many cures and commanded such respect from the people.

Many patriots were still dreaming of the resurgence of Israel as a major power, and Jesus stood out as prime candidate to lead the effort. He was, in many ways, the answer to their prayers. He was just what they wanted. Just what Israel needed: The New King!

Convinced he was just what their world needed at this moment, they abandoned the thought of going straight home, and instead turned back to persuade Jesus to come with them to be crowned king. But he knew what they had in mind. He had sent the apostles across the sea to Capharnaum and, given the tension in the air, they happily piled into their boats and took off. He was alone.

Rather than debate the future of the state of Israel with this throng of well wishers, Jesus took advantage of the darkness and retreated further into the wilderness. They searched for him, but he had disappeared. "Where did he go," they cried. "He was right here just a minute ago."

His disappearance only convinced them all the more that he was indeed the prophet who had been foretold and who would rebuild Israel. They searched intently, but in vain. They would find him no matter what it might take. Maybe not today, but someday. When darkness fell they gave up and headed for home.

After they left, Jesus looked around for a boat, but couldn't find any. The apostles had taken them all. They were already halfway across the water and out of sight. With a little grin, he decided to walk. He had to move fast as they had a pretty good head start. Fortunately, as the Son of God, he could go as fast as he wanted.

As he glided across the water, Jesus noticed a sudden sharp stir in the calm evening air. He detected a storm coming up and hoped the apostles had already reached the other side. He knew they would be scared if there was a storm; it had happened before, and he had to rescue them. He didn't want to have to do it again. They were going to have to learn to shift for themselves someday; he wouldn't always be on hand to bail them out.

And so it was. The apostles' boats were nowhere near the shore of Capharnaum. Land had just come into view, but the sight of it was quickly erased by a violent downpour that darkened the sky even further. Now they couldn't even see where they were going. The wind became a gale and tossed the boats about like toys. Though they were fishermen, and accustomed to storms on the water, they had never seen anything like this. They were soaked and they were in peril of their lives.

Not one of them thought of Jesus, and where he was and how he was getting along in the storm. They presumed he was following them in another boat, not realizing that they had taken them all, leaving none for their leader. But he was making good time on the water as the wind and rain parted as he came through.

The apostles had enough trouble just keeping afloat without worrying where Jesus was. They did the best they could to keep the boats upright but the waves were crashing so violently that they were about ready to give up and try to swim to shore. But, how could they swim in these waves? And, where's the shore anyway? They were afraid they were going in circles. Maybe the storm would dissipate soon. It was their only hope. But the howling wind and crashing seas continued and even intensified.

Then they knew they were done for. In the middle of this tempest, the wind whipping at their faces, the rain pelting them like tiny needles, they feared they were losing their minds. They started seeing things.

A ghost suddenly appeared in the darkness! It was walking! On the water, floating effortlessly towards them. Their frantic screams penetrated even the roar of the wind and the crashing of the waves.

But then the ghost spoke: "Don't be afraid. It is I, Jesus." And he continued walking, totally unbothered by the torrent that was driving them crazy. The apostles cried out in fear as Jesus came nearer to the boat. Peter seemed doubtful and said, "If it is really you, Lord, tell me to come out there and walk to you."

And Jesus said "Come."

Peter looked around at the other apostles as if to say, "Can you believe this?" But he pumped up his courage and got out of the boat into the storm and the crashing waves and howling wind, and began to walk toward Jesus.

"I'm doing it" he said to himself. "I'm really walking on the water!" The other apostles watched with a combination of awe and apprehension.

Soon enough, however, Peter began to question how this could happen, how he could get out of the boat in the middle of the sea and actually walk upon the water, just as Jesus was doing! How is it possible?

As his rational mind took over his sense of faith began to crumble, and he, as a result, began to go under. "Lord, save me!" he cried out. Calmly, Jesus reached out his hand and pulled him out of the water.

And as he did so, the winds immediately quieted and the waters calmed. Once again, Jesus had saved them and controlled the wind and waves. He helped Peter get back into the boat.

As a soggy Peter lay in the bottom of the boat, he relived what had just happened. He had walked on the water. He had done it! He didn't know how it was possible, but maybe he didn't need to know. Maybe it didn't matter if he understood how Jesus did these things. He was amazed at himself that he had actually stepped out of the boat when Jesus called him. What was he thinking?

It made no rational sense for an uneducated fisherman to get out of a boat in the middle of a storm and think he really could walk on water. But he did!

Peter still did not grasp the fact that it was precisely because it made no rational sense that it made all the sense in the world. Jesus opened his eyes with his own commentary on the event. Peter's entire being ached when he heard him say "Why did you have so little faith in me?"

Faith! It was his faith in Jesus that let him do it, not his meager understanding of the surface tension of water in a violent storm. And, it was exactly when his rational mind began to question his faith that he began to sink.

He winced as Jesus asked "Why did you doubt me? Is your faith still so weak." Peter's face was now soaked by his own tears as much as by the waters of the sea. He grasped Jesus' hands and cried "You are indeed the Son of God!"

When I heard this story, for word of it got around pretty quickly, a certain set of coincidences struck me. It seemed Jesus had a special thing about water. It seemed very important to him for some reason that was not immediately obvious to me.

First there was the scene with John at the River Jordan. John had earned his nickname "The Baptist," through his ritualistic dunking of sinners into the waters, which, I believe, symbolized the washing away of their sins and failings and giving them a new birth, a second chance, so to speak, to amend their lives.

Then there was that embarrassing occurrence at Cana, where Jesus saved the wedding party from disaster by turning water into top-quality wine. That was the first of his many miracles and still my favorite because it was very good wine.

I also recalled the situation with the Samaritan woman at the well in Sichar. This is when it really started getting confusing, with Jesus talking about a special kind of water that would eliminate thirst forever for those who drank it and lead to eternal life.

And it was at the waters of Sheepgate pond that he cured a poor helpless man who had been hoping for thirty eight years to be made whole. Then there were the storms and calming of the waters. While the Apostles were in fear for their lives he had no trouble with water, no matter how turbulent. He even walked on it. Yes, it seemed to me that Jesus really liked water, but I sure couldn't figure out why.

I couldn't get these many coincidences with water out of my head. But then I remembered a busy crowded place a long, long time ago and a young couple on a donkey with no place to stay. And I remembered a man coming up and asking me for a little water for his wife, the mom of a newborn child, a boy named Jesus. My mind reeled at the memory.

Is it possible Jesus knows that I was the one who was in Bethlehem that night and that I was willing to help Joseph? Does he know that I was at his birthplace and heard all the singing and saw the animals and shepherds and kings and felt the incredible peace? Does he know that because of that night I have made him my life's quest and that I would do anything for him? Is that cup of water I gave Joseph the magic ticket that allows me admission as a special witness of all these events? Is it possible that Jesus might know who I am?

Of course he does. He is the Son of God. He knows everything. I was convinced of that. I bet he even knows I'm storing this diary in a water jug.

The Gift of Sight

> And immediately he was able to see, and followed Jesus glorifying God. And all the people who saw this also gave praise to God. Luke 18.43

I WAS PART OF a crowd one day just outside of Jericho that had gathered due to a rumor that Jesus would be passing by. And not surprisingly, as the day wore on, the crowd grew, lining the street for miles.

Everybody was there, at least everybody who was hoping to get something from Jesus: the blind, the poor, the deaf, the paralytic, the beggars, the sick and those missing limbs, and far off to the side, as required by law, the lepers. All hoping to see Jesus and to be cured by him.

This was not a quiet crowd. There was quite a bit of shouting and jostling as people strived to be in a good position to see Jesus and to be seen by Jesus. But not everybody could be in the front line as the crowd was now several layers deep, and kept growing with every passing minute.

Finally Jesus came into view; he was just rounding the corner. Several of his key apostles were with him. They kept trying to control the crowd and prevent them from crushing Jesus in their mad rush to greet him.

In contrast to the excitement of the crowd Jesus was perfectly calm. Some people knelt as he walked by; others attempted to reach out to touch him, for it was well known that at least one person had been cured simply by touching his cloak. Others cried out to grab his attention, and he would occasionally turn to face such a petitioner to ask what they wanted.

In most cases it was obvious. The blind wanted to see; the ailing to be well again; the lame to walk; the deaf to hear; and the lepers made clean. I think by asking them Jesus was trying to measure the depth of their faith, rather than confirm what everybody could already see. He wasn't just showing off by curing people, he was trying to convince them of who he really was: the Son of God, rather than just a superpower magician. For him, faith was more important than anything else.

It was getting really loud. One blind beggar in particular was trying to outshout the crowd all by himself. His rich baritone was booming out at Jesus, even though he couldn't see him. He had been here hours before the crowd began to assemble, as this was where he usually parked himself to beg for alms. He thought he was going to have a good day as the crowd continued to grow but then realized he was not the reason why all these people were here.

So he had asked what was going on. Upon learning that Jesus of Nazareth, the great healer, might be coming through, he began to crank up the volume, shouting "Jesus, Son of David, have mercy on me!" People told him to shut up, but that only made him more desperate and he shouted even louder.

When Jesus came nearer he could not help but hear the guy, who was now just about shredding his vocal cords in desperation. Jesus stopped his caravan and asked for the man to be brought to the front to he could see him. The crowd parted as the beggar was led forward. Jesus asked his name and learned it was Bartimeus. Someone said that this is where he usually could be found begging practically every day. Anyone could tell that he was blind.

But then Jesus asked the question that always puzzled me: "What would you like me to do for you?" Bartimeus, however, did not seem disappointed at the question, and replied quickly and in a confident voice: "Rabbi, I want to be able to see." Jesus said: "Because of your faith, your eyes will be made open. You can go on your way." Bartimeus blinked, looked around with amazement as the real world came into focus, and smiled broadly. His wish had been granted and his life would never be the same. But instead of going on this way he joined the crowd, using his powerful voice to praise the one who had healed him.

That was just one of the cures of blind people that I saw Jesus perform. There were many others. One in particular really puzzled me. Actually it involved two blind men, but the circumstances were familiar. They were following Jesus, crying out with the words: "Have pity on us, Son of David." Finally, they attracted his attention and he stopped to deal with their problem.

Now this is where it differed from his usual routine. He did not ask them what they wanted him to do for them. It was obvious that they were blind. Instead, he went right to the core of the matter by asking them "Do you believe that I really have the power to make you see?" He was quite directly questioning their faith to see if it was real. They did not disappoint: "Yes, Lord, we believe you do." And, because of their strong faith, their wish was granted. They looked at Jesus with eyes wide with gratitude.

But now it got even more confusing, so confusing that I began to question what it was that Jesus really wanted to accomplish with all these miracles. For, after restoring their sight, he told them quite sternly that they were to tell no one what happened. In other words, let it be our little secret. I thought that request would be impossible for them to obey.

First of all, they could not keep a secret of their sudden ability to see. People were going to notice, and say, "Hey, didn't you guys used to be blind?" Word would get out that they who were formerly blind could now see, and people were going to wonder how it happened. Furthermore, you cannot reasonably expect people who are thoroughly elated at their sudden gift of sight to keep quiet about it.

And, in fact, they did not keep quiet about it. Instead they shouted from the rooftops, eager to tell one and all just what the Son of David had done for them. As a result, his notoriety grew exponentially, as more and more people learned what happened.

Here's what confused me even further: How, and why, did Jesus expect to shove these actions under the rug? How could he rationally expect people who were so miraculously cured of blindness to not want to tell the world about their good fortune?

He was a man just like they were, with the same human emotions, so he had to know that what he was asking of them was a virtual impossibility. Nobody, no matter how disciplined, could do it. I doubt even Jesus himself, had he been the recipient of such a great benefit, could keep it under wraps.

I was also bothered by the question: Why? Did he not tell his apostles not to hide their light under a bushel? Did he not call them the Light of the World and the Salt of the Earth? Such things are not easily hidden. I was so confused and disappointed that I began to doubt if Jesus was really serious about what he was doing.

How could he expect to restore the kingdom of God in the world of Israel if it did not become immediately quite clear to all concerned that he really was the Son of God? Why was he hiding his lamp under a bushel? I thought it was, at the very least, counterproductive.

I was not the only one confused by this. I could see it in the faces of the apostles. Their faith was not necessarily any stronger than the man in the street, a fact that had caused Jesus considerable consternation on many occasions. Peter, being the Rock that he is, put up a good front and tried to be an example to the other guys. But his faith was weak.

I began to wonder if Jesus had changed his mind about this whole deal. Maybe he really wanted to just go away in the desert and take up the lifestyle of his cousin John. I smiled inwardly at the thought of Jesus in a camel skin cloak and eating grasshoppers!

I think things would have been better all around if Jesus had chosen me to be on his team, instead of some of these other guys. Especially Judas the money manager. I still didn't like his looks.

Or maybe there was another kind of blindness and I was suffering from it. Maybe my eyes needed to be opened too. Maybe there was a big picture out there that I just hadn't seen yet. Maybe, if I continued following Jesus, he could cure me too.

The Ultimate Curse

> "Lord, if you want to, you can make me clean." And Jesus, extending his hand, touched him and said: "I want to." And immediately he was cleansed of his leprosy. Matthew 8.2

ONE DAY, I was following Jesus as he and several of his apostles were on their way to Jerusalem. It was a nice day, warm, but not overbearing, a good day to be on the road. Just as the group was about to enter a small village near Samaria we heard riotous yelling and cursing.

Villagers were chasing a group of lepers out of town. I counted ten of them, hobbling as quickly as they could to avoid the stones and rotten vegetables being thrown at them. Because of their dreadful disease, lepers were not welcome in this village, or anywhere else.

They were considered unclean; they were shunned, cursed and isolated, true outcasts, welcome virtually nowhere. There was no hope for them. The disease was unstoppable. Its progress was tragic. At first, the victims gradually became numb in their extremities, so that they could not feel pain.

Rather than a benefit, this was the kiss of death because they were often unaware of small cuts and lacerations that later would cause infections and the loss of toes, fingers or even one of their limbs. Their bodies were scarred with a horrible, painful rash. There was the smell of putrefaction as their bodies slowly rotted away.

I couldn't figure out how these lepers got into the village in the first place. They usually were very careful to huddle together in pitiable groups and stay away from other people. They knew they would be driven away once they were identified. To be near a leper was very dangerous, as the disease was considered highly contagious and most people, including me, lived in fear of it. That's why the ancient laws required them to cry out "Unclean, unclean!" whenever they came near another person.

Many towns and villages had a ghetto outside the walls where lepers would be allowed to gather. They relied on relatives or friends for the basic necessities of life, something to eat or a bit of clothing but, for the most part, they were on their own. Many were forced to become beggars, attempting to conceal their deformities so as not to be recognized as a leper and chased out of town.

No one really knew why the disease would strike one and not another. But the Pharisees had the answer: sin. They felt they had the answer to everything, it seemed to me. As far as they were concerned, whenever there was illness, injury or suffering, sin was always the cause. On one occasion, when Jesus was about to cure a blind man, they asked him outright whether his blindness was the result of his sins or his parents'?

Jesus told them sin was not the issue, but that these maladies occurred so he could demonstrate his power to cure bodily ailments and, by extension, forgive sins also. I began to wonder just how horrendous one's sins would have to be, in the Pharisees' reckoning, to deserve the ultimate punishment of leprosy.

The lepers eventually saw Jesus and began calling out to him: "Jesus, Son of David, save us!" Jesus was his usual calm self. I thought he would just ask them what they wanted as he always did, even though everybody knew they would want to be healed. They were raising quite a ruckus, yelling at the top of their lungs.

They had to stay at a distance for fear of being chased away, but that was no problem. Their external bodies may have been a mess but their lungs were strong, so they cried out ever louder and louder, "Jesus, have pity on us." People were starting to pick up rocks and telling them to shut up, but they were not going to let the opportunity to be touched by Jesus pass them by without a struggle.

I wasn't sure how he was going to handle this. Would he just go ahead and cure all ten of them? Or would he first try to measure their faith and then cure only those who met his standards? But how could he turn away those whose faith was weak? I glanced at the apostles who were with Jesus and recalled how he had frequently chastised them for their lack of faith even after all he had done. This might prove to be a lesson for them.

Once again Jesus surprised me. For he did not ask them what they wanted him to do. He did not ask if they believed he could cure them. Jesus motioned for the lepers to step forward. They quieted down and took a few halting steps toward Jesus.

But before they got even halfway he told them: "Be on your way. Go show yourselves to the priests." They took off, hobbling along on weakened and unfeeling legs. Soon though, their speed increased as the symptoms of the dreaded disease gradually disappeared from their bodies.

That was it? No measuring the depth of their faith? No questions or admonitions or warnings? Jesus was always surprising me. And I think he surprised his apostles as well, as they looked at one another with a mixture of puzzlement and wonder, as if to say "Can you believe that?"

When the ten lepers had disappeared from view, Jesus and his entourage continued on their way to Jerusalem. They had not gone very far, however, when they were met by an obviously cheerful fellow prancing along all by himself. I didn't know who he was, but he sure seemed happy. Jesus recognized him at once as one of the ten lepers he had cured. Right in the middle of the road the man fell down flat on his face at the feet of Jesus and, with tears running down his face, cried out his thanks.

Jesus was obviously moved by this heartfelt expression of gratitude. But then, he looked around as if surveying the surrounding area. There was a measure of disappointment in his gaze. He shook his head and asked: "Didn't I cure ten lepers? Where are the rest of them, the other nine?"

Of course the man did not have an answer for that question. He just kept crying out his thanks to God. Noticing that he was a Samaritan, Jesus remarked that, out of the ten who were made clean, only this foreigner understood what really happened, and he came back to give thanks and declare his belief in Jesus.

As we all stood there wondering, Jesus wrapped it up in a nutshell, saying to the man who still lay prostrate and crying at his feet: "Get up now. Your faith is what has cured you." The man hopped to his feet, delighted with his new-found health and dreaming of becoming a normal member of society. He never stopped praising Jesus as he danced off, his voice gradually fading away as he disappeared down the road.

Faith. So there it was, again. Faith in Jesus as the Son of God and forgiver of sins is what made all the difference. Sure, the other nine had been made whole, but this man, a foreigner, was the only one who exhibited the level of belief that Jesus was seeking.

In a sense, it was the same story over and over. Despite the miraculous cures and great signs and wonders and accomplishments, faith was all that mattered to Jesus. Faith was what made all this happen. Faith, I think, was the end and aim of everything he did.

I ran ahead to catch up with the now-cured leper. I wanted to learn more about his life and what this cure would mean to him. Recognizing me as someone who had been with Jesus, he wrapped his arms around me and shouted thanks right into my ear. At first I tried to pull back, but then I realized he wasn't a leper any more. Maybe that was a test of my faith, to see if I really believed Jesus had cured him. I did not doubt it at all.

"I'm going home to see my family," he said. "That's the most important and first thing I want to do. I have had this illness for ten years. It has ruined my life, our lives, really, because my family is also looked down upon due to my leprosy. The Pharisees say our whole family is guilty of sin and that is what caused me to get sick. But I don't believe it. We never did anything wrong."

He continued: "Do you have any idea what it's like to have perfect strangers throw rocks at you the minute they see you? I became an instant object of everyone's hatred. I had an overpowering feeling of complete worthlessness. I began to ask myself what I had done to deserve this. People asked what sin had I committed to be struck with this painful and disgusting illness, but I couldn't think of anything I had done that was so terribly wrong. I cried myself to sleep almost every night. I even wanted to kill myself."

"The pain must have been unbearable," I said. He answered, "It wasn't the physical pain. It was the crushing sense of loneliness. The ten of us who were separated in that compound outside the walls never talked to anyone else, never saw anyone else. We were in a permanent quarantine. As if our bodily ailment wasn't enough, we were losing our minds over the isolation and loneliness. The hardest part was knowing that no one, no one, was ever going to come looking for you, never ask about you nor even care if you're alive or dead. You might as well be dead. I wished I was."

Impulsively, he hugged me again, saying "What Jesus did for me by curing my body is nothing compared to what he did for my soul. I was as good as dead. He has brought me back to life!"

When we broke our embrace, I saw that he was in tears. And so was I.

Throwing Stones

> However, one after another they began to walk away, beginning with the oldest, until Jesus was left alone with the woman in the middle of the temple. John 8.9

DESPITE JESUS' OUTSTANDING accomplishments for the benefit of needy and hurting people, he was a consistent object of scorn and derision in the eyes of the Pharisees and local political leaders. The reason was obvious. He was challenging them, questioning their authority and diminishing their influence. Furthermore, he seemed to have no respect or awe for their positions of power. He usually ignored them, but on at least one occasion he told them what he thought of them in clear, uncertain terms.

He called them hypocrites and made fun of their practice of grandstanding their humility and religiosity, wearing sad faces when they fasted, but still seeking the best seats at banquets and parties. He called them blind guides. He said they were doomed. He called them whitened sepulchers, gold-plated caskets that look pretty on the outside but are filled with decay and filth within.

Rather than heed what Jesus was saying and possibly change their ways, they decided the only solution was to do away with him. They could not win any argument with him or solve any of the conundrums he placed before them. When their power was challenged in this way they did not turn to logical argument to prove their point. On the contrary, their only response was violence.

One particular confrontation concerned a woman who had been caught in adultery. She was brought into the square by the Scribes and Pharisees and thrown to the ground before Jesus. They thought they had him in this case, as it was clear what should be done with such a wanton woman.

Contrary to his law of forgiveness and accommodation, the law of Moses said she should be stoned to death for her transgression. Would he go against the law and suggest that lenience should be shown to someone so demonstrably guilty of serious sin? Their trap seemed inescapable, even for Jesus. Their hearts throbbed with excitement as they expected a victory, at last.

The potential for a public stoning usually attracted a large crowd and this was no exception. I just happened to be walking by and so I stopped to watch.

The accused woman lay cowering on the ground, her hands over her head, providing pitiable protection against the rocks and other projectiles that were expected to begin pelting her any second. She sobbed, her tears betraying not only her guilt but also her fear of pain and death.

But the accusers seemed in no hurry to exact the severe punishment this pathetic woman deserved. First they wanted to prove a point with Jesus, to see if they could catch him on the wrong side of the law.

They called him "Rabbi," with phony respect. A little chuckling and giggling could be heard in the background, so sure were they that Jesus could not possibly have an answer to the dilemma they were about to propose.

"This woman has been caught in the act of committing adultery. There is no question she is guilty. She knows it; we know it; the whole world knows it." Jesus looked at them with an attitude of "So What?" on his face. They continued: "According to the Law, we are told by Moses that such a woman should be put to death by stoning."

Jesus continued looking at them quizzically, as if to say "Just how does this concern me?" They were getting upset that he was not getting upset. The giggling and chuckling had quickly stopped. Finally, after a few more moments, their patience was gone, and one of them shouted. "All right, that's what the law says and what Moses says! What do you say?"

Jesus ignored their question. Instead, he stooped down and started drawing something in the dust. I couldn't tell what it was. But I could tell they were frustrated and angered by the fact that he was not taking their bait and venturing an answer to their question. So, a couple of them came forward and raised their voices. "Look, we asked you a question and we want an answer! Now! You have a great following among the people. We have a right to know what you think."

Jesus just kept drawing pictures on the ground. I was getting curious about what type of art he was creating.

Now a few more Pharisees gathered around him and shouted angrily: "Do you agree with Moses or not?" said one. "It's a simple question!" shouted another, "Yes or no?"

Jesus looked up, seemingly surprised at their agitation, and said: "I would suggest that, if there is anyone among you who is totally without sin, it would be all right for that person to throw a stone at her." Then he continued drawing figures in the dust.

Those standing near him looked down to see what he had drawn. They stared at each other with guilty looks, and then started slowly walking away, shaking their heads. The rest of them also approached Jesus, who was still busy making pictures. They too hung their heads and walked away, dropping their stones with a dull thud when they saw what he had drawn.

When they all had left, Jesus asked the woman, who was still trembling on the ground, still expecting to feel the pain of flying rocks: "What happened to the people who were accusing you? Are they all gone?"

Obviously relieved, she looked around, her eyes red with tears. "I don't think there's anybody here to condemn me any more," she sobbed. "Then I don't condemn you either," he said. "Get up. Go home. And sin no more." Jesus extended a hand to help her get to her feet, and she went on her way, shaken by the experience but thankful to be alive.

I saw the Pharisees grumbling among themselves. They looked ready to pick up stones to throw at Jesus. They had failed again. He had outsmarted them again. After they all walked away, I sidled over to where Jesus had been to see what he was drawing that had so upset them.

He wasn't drawing pictures. He was writing, and I think I understood why no stones were thrown that day. In the dust I could read "Thief," "Liar," "Cheat," "Embezzler," "Murderer," and "Adulterer."

Lazarus, Come Forth!

Jesus said: "Have I not told you that if only you believe you will see the glory of God?" John 11.40

THE ILLNESS OF Lazarus struck Jesus especially hard. Jesus was usually quite indiscriminate when it came to helping people. It made no difference who required his assistance. He cured or helped virtually all who came to him, usually more concerned with the seriousness and depth of their faith than their particular ailment. Faith was what he really was seeking and was often the deciding factor in the miracles he performed. But Lazarus was different. He was his friend; and his sickness touched Jesus personally.

Lazarus and his two sisters, Martha and Mary, lived in Bethany. The three siblings were very close to each other and to Jesus.

What seemed strange to me was that, when Mary and Martha told Jesus that his old friend was ill, he did not immediately speed over to Bethany to be with him. In fact, I heard he waited a full two days before setting out. I thought this was no problem, as he had previously cured people on several occasions without actually going to see them. There was no need for him to be physically present with Lazarus in order to work his miraculous powers.

Bethany was in Judea, where it was well known that the Pharisees were on the lookout for Jesus. His arrival there would stir up a hornet's nest of hatred that could only end badly for him.

Nevertheless, after waiting two days, he announced to his disciples that they were going there, no matter what.

They immediately raised a torrent of reasons against the journey, wisely pointing out that the Pharisees had already tried to stone him to death there and were surely anxious for another chance to finish him off.

But Jesus said, "Our friend has fallen asleep; and I have to go wake him up." Puzzled, the disciples asked "Well, if he's just asleep, what's the problem? Why go risk your life and limb if he's just napping and will wake up sooner or later anyway?" What they didn't understand, and what Jesus knew, was the fact that Lazarus was already dead.

Jesus said "Look, I didn't mean he was just napping. I was talking about the sleep of death. We are going to go there and I will bring him back to life so you will believe that I have the power to do so."

Despite further arguments about the death trap he was entering by going to see his friend, they all took off, willing to risk their own lives along with Jesus their leader. I think it was Thomas who said "We might all be killed, but let's go with him." I got wind of the fact that they were leaving and attached myself to their little group so I could see Jesus in action once again.

But even before we drew near to Bethany word had already gotten to Martha that Jesus was on his way. She left Mary at home and rushed out to meet him. We were just a few miles from town when she appeared, covered in tears of both grief for her dead brother and joy at seeing Jesus. Sadly, she told him that her brother Lazarus had already been dead four days. "But, I know if you had been here he would not have died," she said to Jesus. Her faith in him became obvious to us all when she said "I know God will do whatever you ask of him."

Jesus simply said: "Don't worry, he will rise again." Then he started speaking words that I could understand individually, but which became incomprehensible when positioned together by Jesus. As best I could recall he said "I am the resurrection and the life. Whoever believes in me will live, even if he dies. Anyone who is alive and believes in me will never die."

Now, I knew exactly what each of those words means. They are basic concepts: life, death, belief. But Jesus somehow scrambled them together into a complete riddle. I tried to figure out how someone who dies can still be alive; and, more complex yet, how it can be possible that one will "never" die. Life and death are mutually exclusive concepts. You get one or the other, but you can't have both at the same time. People, animals and trees, and even stones, are either dead or alive. Things that are alive, sooner or later do, in fact, die. But evidently not according to Jesus. Well, he did it again: I was totally confused.

Then he stared at Martha with great seriousness and demanded: "Do you believe this?" With no hesitation whatsoever she replied "Yes! I believe that you are the Messiah, the Son of God!" Without another word she ran off to tell Mary that Jesus was on his way. But before we moved very far, Mary came rushing out to meet us.

She was accompanied by a group of visitors from Jerusalem who had come to mourn Lazarus and who also were eager to see Jesus, having heard that he was in the neighborhood. Even though Martha's reaction to Jesus was one of complete faith, it was nothing compared to Mary's. She threw herself down at his feet, her eyes filled with tears. In fact, the interaction between the two of them was so loving and touching that I think everyone's eyes were overflowing at this point.

She cried, "Lord, if only you had been here, my brother would not have died." I don't think she meant this as a complaint, but more as an expression of her faith in Jesus. He was obviously touched by her faith, and seeing her at weeping before him, he helped her to her feet and asked "Where is he?"

Then Jesus did something I thought I would never see. He cried. He wept, openly and unashamedly. His tears ran down his cheeks and dampened his beard.

As they neared the tomb it was obvious Jesus was not himself. He was still grievously pained. Although I never thought of him as an emotional guy, he was clearly having trouble keeping it together.

What a paradox! Two minutes ago he was being hailed as the Son of God, the Messiah, now he stood there weeping like a child over the loss of his friend. The Jews who had come with Mary whispered to each other, "He must have really loved him."

My understanding of Jesus now grew even deeper and more complex. He always seemed so godlike and in control, so perfect in word and deed, so…intimidating. Now, seeing this shockingly human side of him, I was filled with admiration, appreciation, and I must say, even love. He was clearly the Son of God.

He had proven that to me dozens of times. But now he had proven himself also to be a real man, with normal emotions and feelings and passions. I appreciated him even more for having seen this side of him. He was more approachable, more like me. I liked that.

The tension was overwhelming as we came closer to the actual tomb. It was a cave with a large stone rolled across the entrance. Jesus said "Take the stone away so he can come out." People were already holding their noses in fearful anticipation of the stench of a four-day old corpse. Now some began backing away from the scene.

"There's going to be a horrible smell!" Martha cried. Jesus replied, "Didn't I tell you that you must have faith in me? Do not doubt that I can do this." Finally some of the men rolled the stone away. Oddly, they did not seem to be affected by any odor of a decomposing body. I was surprised at how difficult it was for the two fully grown men to roll the huge stone aside.

When they had done so, Jesus called out in a loud voice "Lazarus, come forth!" We waited expectantly. Within just a few seconds we saw movement inside the cave. A white-shrouded figure was slowly gliding towards the entrance to the tomb, toward the light of day. Even though it was still wrapped from head to toe in the burial cloths, we were convinced it had to be Lazarus.

Jesus said, "Let's get that shroud off of him, so he can move about." Once Lazarus was free of his wrappings he raced to Jesus, and the two friends fell into a warm and lengthy embrace. Both were in tears.

The reaction of the crowd, especially the visitors from Jerusalem, was complete amazement. Many had heard of Jesus, but now they saw him in action, and they believed in him. They proclaimed him the Son of God. Perhaps some of them might have doubted that he could bring Lazarus back to life. But I didn't. I knew all along he could do it.

Mary and Martha immediately got to work preparing something to eat for Jesus, with an extra helping for Lazarus, who had to be hungry after four days without food. The visitors from Jerusalem joined in as well, grinning and laughing. They had come to Bethany to mourn their friend, and now they were celebrating with him. One of them raised a toast, "To Lazarus, on the happy occasion of his second birthday!"

It was a nice party, and I made some new friends, with whom I spent a lot of time exchanging stories about Jesus and his exploits.

Jesus didn't stay long in Bethany, for word had gotten out that he was in town, and the chief priests and Pharisees were circling like wolves. Rather than rejoicing at the good work he was doing, they were jealous of the attention he was getting. In fact, I heard they had held a special council and issued a death warrant against him. But they would have to wait for another opportunity to seize him.

They wouldn't have to wait long.

Unless You Become...

> Jesus sternly said: "Leave them alone and let them come to me, for of such is the kingdom of heaven!"
> Matthew 19.13

IT WASN'T TOO long after his resurrection of Lazarus that Jesus was preaching to a large group that included many families, complete with children of all ages. Some of the moms and dads brought their offspring to Jesus so he could bless them and cure whatever ailments they might be suffering from. Some of the kids also brought their pets: cats and dogs and birds and even a few goats.

Peter, however, didn't like what he saw. He felt there were real grown-up problems to be solved and that is where Jesus should be concentrating his efforts instead of playing with the kids. He was afraid things might get out of hand. As was so often the case, he was wrong.

Nevertheless, he convinced a couple of the other disciples that it would be a good idea to get the kids out of the way. So they began berating the parents for letting their children get too close to Jesus. After all, they said, sometimes kids were germy, and they didn't want Jesus to catch something because some little urchin sneezed on him. Their hands were often dirty and sometimes they slobbered when they tried to talk.

Matthew agreed with Peter. His structured tax collector's mind craved discipline and order. How else could he levy the right tax on a person's goods if he didn't have clear instructions and an accurate count of the goods involved? The disorderly scene before him upset his logical mind almost as much as it did Peter's.

Not surprisingly, Judas also jumped at the opportunity to play the bad guy. He seemed perfect for the role and was eager to exercise his authority to shoo the little children away from Jesus.

Jesus, on the other hand, was having the time of his life. He had three kids on his lap and another two or three hanging on him. A few others were jumping up and down, eager to get their turn. A shy little girl handed him a bunch of flowers and said "I picked these for you, Jesus. I love you." He thanked her and blessed her. She ran off grinning.

He was laughing uproariously at their childlike enthusiasm and affection. He readily bestowed his blessing on them and on their parents as well. He even blessed the pets, and a laugh went up when a kitten curled up and fell asleep in his lap. A puppy waddled up and started licking his feet. He petted them both with obvious pleasure.

The people surrounding Jesus and his youthful admirers were not pleased when Peter and his posse tried to break up their happy little love fest. I thought there was going to be a scuffle, as voices and, I presume, tempers were rising.

Kids began crying. "I wanna be with Jesus!" sobbed one. "He's a nice man," said another. "Why don'tcha just leave us alone?" said one dad, a large man, almost as burly as Peter. The kitten hopped off Jesus' lap and scampered away, the puppy close behind.

Jesus was in the midst of a most un-godlike giggle when he became aware of what was going on. "Whoa, wait a minute!" he said. "Leave the kids alone! I like them." There was a sudden silence. Jesus broke the silence with a large grin and open arms, visibly inviting the kids to come back to him.

They came rushing and soon engulfed him with hugs and laughter. Peter and Matthew and Judas threw up their hands as if to say "What can we do with him?" But they soon changed their tune and joined in the fun, serving as volunteer ushers to keep the kids in an orderly line and making sure everybody got a chance to sit on Jesus' lap and tell him their stories.

From what I could see, nobody was having more fun than Jesus. He was like a little kid himself, laughing and joking with the children. Well, he had been a little kid once. I clearly remembered an evening long ago when I first glimpsed a very special child in Bethlehem. I was proud of myself for having made the effort to keep an eye on him, and even more proud of the handsome and personable young man that he had become.

When the kids had all had their chance to visit their hero and Jesus was obviously worn out, he became serious. By this time, much of the crowd had left, but there were still a few of us who remained, along with the disciples. As usual he had a few words for them. And as usual, his words were about faith.

"Did you see those little children?" he asked, still grinning from ear to ear. "Did you see their faith and how easily and naturally they expressed their love?" He chuckled softly, as if remembering something particularly funny, and then looked directly at the three amateur gendarmes who wanted to break up the party.

He wagged his finger playfully but then turned serious as he said "I assure you, unless you become like these little children there will be no place for you in my father's house." Peter, Matthew and Judas shared quizzical looks, unsure what he was getting at.

"Look at their faith," he continued. "Their innocence and simplicity, and how naturally they express their affection." When they go to bed at night they are not filled with the worries of the world as you are. In the morning they are eager to start the new day. When they ask mom or dad for a piece of bread they trust that they will not be given a stone or chunk of wood instead. They love life and believe that things will turn out well for them. They enjoy simple pleasures, their cats and dogs and toys.

"Let their childlike faith be an example for you. You should try to be like them. Those who have the faith of children will be the first to enter my father's house, and will be closest to him."

Jesus did not deliver this advice like a harsh criticism or reprimand. Rather, he spoke softly, encouragingly; he sounded almost like a tutor with an especially promising young scholar. His message, as always, was one of belief and trust. Then he burst out laughing again: "Those kids are great. I just love 'em."

A Triumphal Entry

> The Pharisees said to one another: "Can't you see that we are accomplishing nothing? Look, the whole world is following after him!" John 12.19

JERUSALEM WAS AGOG, massively in love with Jesus. When he came riding into town on a donkey it was hardly possible for him to get through the crowds. Everybody wanted to see him, to touch him or be touched by him. By this time there was hardly a person alive who did not know his name. They knew who he was and what he had done and they liked him.

No, they loved him. They loved him for the miracles he had wrought. He had cured their ailments, healed their blindness and cleansed their leprosy. Moreover, they were now more than ever convinced that he was the Promised One, the Messiah, he who would restore Israel as a special people chosen by Yahweh.

Ancient lore and the prophets told of the coming of such a savior. Books had been written about him before anyone even knew his name or what he would look like. Prophetic scribes had written hopeful tomes describing his royal status, the miracles he would perform, and how he would bring the masses together as one glorious nation blessed by God. He would be a king, mighty and feared by his enemies, but beloved by the people he led.

Sure, there were some disconcerting elements to his story. He certainly didn't look like a conqueror or a king. There appeared to be nothing of the warrior about him. Instead he had a quite placid look, more peacemaker than warmonger. But no matter, he was their chosen one and they were more than pleased with him.

Children echoed their parents' enthusiasm, as they sang and strew palm branches before him. "Hosanna, Son of David" they shouted, recalling that greatest king of old. Yes, he was of the family of David and royal blood ran in his veins. His father, the carpenter, was from the house and family of David. Though now somewhat diminished in wealth and prestige, his lineage was unquestioned. He was The One.

As the kids sang their paeans of glory and the grownups congratulated themselves on the good fortune that was soon surely to be theirs, another sector of the population looked on this garish display of adulation and praise with jaundiced eyes. These were the Pharisees, the Scribes, the pompous hypocritical religious leaders who had hated Jesus the moment they first saw him.

As usual, they stood off by themselves, but they were obvious for their glum faces. I saw them, a gaggle of thugs, their bitterness so intense that it hovered about them like a foul miasma. I knew what they were thinking.

It seemed to them that Jesus had worked deliberately to arouse their hatred. There had hardly been an opportunity for him to cross them that he did not take full advantage of. His every word seemed to be directed at them, exposing their falsity, their hypocrisy, and their greed and disdain for the common people. They were adept at speaking from both sides of their mouth at once, of saying one thing and meaning another. They reminded me of Janus, that two-faced Roman god.

They had a particular ability to trap unsuspecting citizens of infractions of the laws of Yahweh, many which they seemed conjure up on the spot just to intimidate a political or religious enemy. Silly little arcane laws were their specialty; they created a certain paranoia among the people, who were never fully certain if they were doing the right thing in the right way. Even the best of intentions was never enough to please these charlatans.

They had tried their best with Jesus, tossing some of their most complicated conundrums before him. But he was totally unfazed. Always. Whether the question concerned the legality of divorce, or marrying one's brother's widow, or paying taxes to Caesar, or curing on the Sabbath, or ritualistic hand washing, he had the answer. Or he posed an opposition scenario for them that they knew would trap them in a lie or inconsistency.

And so they stood there, seething, in sharp contrast to the rest of the people, who were adoring their Messiah. And it was this contrast that cut them most deeply. Jesus was soaking up all the glory and love and praise and homage and they were being ignored. No one was paying attention to them. No one was singing their praises. No one was tossing palm branches their way.

Instead, people turned their backs on them, even jostled them to get a better view of their hero, to be closer to him and maybe even touch him. Though they maintained an outwardly placid appearance, inwardly their pride roared.

They wanted revenge. The situation was untenable. Outrageous. Jesus had defied them for the last time. They would get even. They would find a way. There had to be some way to reach him where he was most vulnerable. He was only one person, they were many, many of the best and brightest minds in Israel, and the most devious.

All he had was that little band of misfits that followed him around like sheep. Their leader was the biggest joke of all, full of bluster with nothing to back it up. What a rock, as they called him. More like a pebble.

As they slyly pondered this honorary parade for Jesus, a small isolated thought began to develop. Maybe Peter wasn't foolish enough to be tricked into turning on his leader. Well, maybe he was foolish enough, but he was still faithful to Jesus. That was obvious.

But maybe, just maybe, there was a weak link in the group. Maybe one of them had become disenchanted with the message Jesus was peddling. Maybe one of them could be reached, somehow. Maybe one of his chosen few would be willing to rat on Jesus.

But the question remained, which one?

Face to Face with Judas

He gave the bread to Judas, the son of Simon Iscariot. And after just one bite Satan entered into him. John 13.27

IT WAS A few days later that I ran into Judas. He seemed to be in a hurry, making a beeline for the temple. There was a crazy sort of intensity in his eyes as he rushed along. I had met him before and we had seen each other dozens of times. I was on speaking terms with almost all the apostles, except Peter and John. And, of course, I had never spoken to Jesus. Because he was keeper of the purse, Judas was the most recognized member of the group, as he was always bustling about getting provisions and making arrangements for Jesus and his team.

So I figured Judas was on some shopping expedition, probably getting some last-minute supplies for the Passover dinner. I think a few shops were still open. We just exchanged a quick glance and brief nod of recognition and he was on his way. I went on my way too, which included a stop at the local inn for a bite to eat and a cup of wine.

It was a couple hours later when I emerged from the inn, full and slightly lightheaded from a little too much wine. Ever since the miracle at Cana wine has tasted very good to me, though I have yet to find any as excellent as what Jesus produced. But I keep trying.

No sooner did I walk out the door than I ran into Judas again. The second time tonight! What a coincidence, I thought. But now he seemed really disheveled and wild. I was afraid there was something wrong with him, so I asked him if he was okay. I have to admit I never really liked the guy because of his shady looks, but I figured if he was in trouble the least I could do would be to offer some assistance.

So I asked him if he was hungry. The inn was still open and the food was good and plentiful and maybe that's what he needed. So I reentered the inn with Judas at my side. No sooner did we sit down than he buried his face in his hands and began sobbing uncontrollably. I had never seen a man so distraught. Some folks were beginning to look our way. I asked what was the matter.

"It's all his fault," he croaked between sobs. "It didn't have to be this way." I asked what he meant by that. Little did I know that I was opening the door to a whole immense world of frustration, anxiety and guilt. And it was all about Jesus. As best I can recall, as I had already ordered another cup of wine, this is what he had to say.

He said he was afraid that Jesus was a fraud. He was not going to become a real king. He was not going to lead Israel to greatness. He was not going to be another David. He was never going to assemble a mighty army. He was making strange statements, like his kingdom was not of this world. Not only that, but rather than being crowned king and worshipped by all his people, he was going to suffer and die a horrible death. He told us all this, Judas said.

I couldn't believe it. I said, "Judas, you have been with him from the beginning. You have seen him in action up close, standing right at his side. How can you even think this way?"

"I'm telling you what he said," he replied. "We were all talking about it the other day. It all started with Zebedee's wife, the mother of James and John, two of the apostles. She had a special request." Then he added in a childish singsong voice: "Please Jesus, when you establish your kingdom, can my two little boys please sit at your right hand and left hand?" He smirked. "I thought she was totally out of line and so did the other guys, but her two kids were taking it seriously and started arguing about it."

I asked "Isn't Peter the number one guy?" "Of course he is," Judas said, "but that's not the point. We all thought about what the future might hold for us. But, when Jesus heard that we were wondering about the great and glorious roles we might play in his reign, he really blew up at us."

Judas continued, "'Look,' Jesus said, 'I've been telling you guys from the very beginning that my job is not to establish an earthly kingdom, but rather to pave the way for the world to heal its relationship with my Father in heaven. We are hoping to establish a new covenant, one that hopefully mankind will honor this time. I am getting tired of doing all the work while mankind still is hard-headed and will not believe. I'm tired of it and so is my Father. That's why he sent me. That's why I have to suffer and die. For you.'"

I didn't know what to make of all this. On the one hand, Judas was out of his mind. Whether it was due to disappointment with what Jesus was saying or with his own lack of advancement on the team, or the mundane responsibilities with which he was burdened, he was clearly not thinking rationally. Had he misunderstood what Jesus was saying, or was Jesus talking in one of those curious parables of his again, which hardly anyone ever understood without him explaining it?

I asked him about the other guys. "They believe in him!" he shouted. It was suddenly very quiet; now everyone was looking at us. Judas slinked down in his chair. When the noise level grew back to normal he sat up and continued. "He convinced Peter first of all, and then John. Those two are the real leaders. They're complete opposites as personalities. Peter is gruff and no-nonsense, intense to the nth degree; while John is a real smooth character, persuasive and persistent in an unassuming way. They convinced the rest of the guys."

"But what about you?" I asked. "I'm not going to be taken in by all this holy talk of covenants and resurrection and all that," he replied.

"Resurrection?" I querried.

"That's where it really gets weird." Judas said.

Resurrection?

> He will be betrayed and mocked and flogged and spit upon. Then he will be killed, and on the third day he will rise again. Luke 18.31

"RESURRECTION?" I ASKED again. Judas suddenly seemed even more nervous than before. His eyes flashed like shooting stars. His nostrils flared and, for a moment at least, it seemed to me that his whole visage began to change into something almost diabolic.

"Yes!" he replied, with a level of intensity that I had never before experienced in a human being. "We were sitting there, enjoying our meal, when he started talking nonsense about what is really going to happen to him, and us. No kingdom, no royalty, no high positions for those of us who have dedicated our lives to him. No sitting at his right hand for James or John, or any of us in fact!"

I had to admit that did sound disappointing. But then, I really didn't know what to expect, as I had never been in any of these secret meetings with Jesus.

Judas continued: "We sat there looking at each other with puzzled faces. We weren't expecting this. A couple of the guys were nodding their heads as if they knew what he was talking about. You know, Peter, John and a few others. Thomas looked doubtful and so was I.

"But he just kept going on about how he was going to suffer and die, and after that, how we would be persecuted and maybe even killed also. He said that the ancient writings of the prophets foretold all this, that people should have known that he was coming and what he was all about."

I recalled Jesus saying that those who suffer persecution for his sake would have a great reward in heaven, and reminded Judas of that promise.

He exploded with laughter: "Promises, promises, promises, that's all we ever got! Promise of what?" he cried. "That we will be hunted like animals, suffer persecution and die painful deaths, all for the dream of an unknown reward in a fictitious place called heaven?" He laughed again.

"He explained that all the ancient writers and prophets foretold what the so-called Messiah would have to go through. Maybe so, but most people who have read that stuff still think the Messiah is going to establish a kingdom and smash all our enemies so we can live in peace at last. Now, he's telling us the exact opposite, that there definitely will be no great restoration of our land, and that it will be just a spiritual kingdom instead."

Judas stopped for a moment to take a sip of wine. He was either totally mad or drunk, or, I was repelled by the thought, possessed. Suddenly he blurted out: "You saw all those people out there when he made his triumphal entry into Jerusalem! You heard all that singing and shouts of praise. Well, guess what! Jesus says those people who wanted to crown him king are going to turn against him in a matter of days, and before you know it, will be demanding he be put to death!"

I said I didn't see how that was possible, but Judas never stopped talking. "Then, after he is killed, he is going to come back to life. The resurrection!" he shouted, standing up and raising his glass as if giving a toast. Now everyone was looking our way. He sat down, took a sip of wine, and continued in a low voice: "The whole scheme has been put together by the Pharisees, along with some other malcontents he has rubbed the wrong way."

I thought of the moneychangers in the temple and others who had been embarrassed or outwitted by Jesus. On many occasions I had seen the Pharisees huddled together, snickering among themselves, outwardly laughing but inwardly burning with hatred for this man. They were a pack of wolves circling their prey. The thought sent a chill through me, as I began to realize Judas might be right, that these people really were that vindictive and cruel.

"When will all this take place?" I asked, attempting to quiet him down a bit. I was hoping he simply had misunderstood what Jesus was talking about. "Soon," was all he said, with a slight nod of understanding. "Soon."

Then, with a sneer, he added, "You can't imagine the power of pure hatred. They will do anything. Anything. I've been approached several times by people whose names I will not mention. We all have been, I think, at one time or another. We never really talked about it, but it was there. And why not? We're the only ones who know his plans and whereabouts at all times."

I was beginning to feel very uncomfortable, and wished I had not invited Judas to join me in the inn. The wine was getting to him and he was talking very freely, expressing his disappointment now that his dreams of a high position, perhaps treasurer in the new realm, were shattered. It was rumored that he had pilfered funds from the purse he was responsible for, and I could imagine how much graft he could be capable of given a larger opportunity.

Then he said "Don't you see? The tension and fear are starting to get to him. He's always been a little strange, but now he's talking nonsense."

"Is the thought of a kingdom of heaven and a new covenant nonsense?" I asked. "That's not what I'm talking about!" he shouted. I wished he would quiet down, but he was out of control. Lowering his voice, he continued: "Do you remember the time, several years ago, when he got into an argument over his tantrum in the temple when he knocked over the money changers' table and all that? So the Pharisees challenged him and he said he could destroy that temple and build a new one in three days?"

I nodded. Of course I remembered that event. Who could forget it? "Well," Judas said with a smirk, "Now he says that he wasn't talking about an actual temple made of wood and stone. No, he was talking about the temple of his body. His body is a temple, get it?"

I shook my head. I didn't get it. "That's where this idea of resurrection comes in," Judas said. "He claims that he will be killed somehow and by somebody, and he will be buried. But after three days he will come back to life! He will be resurrected! He will walk amongst us again, as if nothing had happened. When he said he would rebuild the temple in three days he wasn't talking about the big building in Jerusalem. He was talking about his body, his life!"

I was in awe. Everything began to make sense. He truly was the Son of God. I was now more convinced of that fact than ever. This would prove it to the world. If he could raise Lazarus from the dead, and the centurion's servant and the son of the royal official, he certainly could raise himself from the dead.

"Don't you believe that he is the Son of God?" I asked Judas. "You are one of his chosen ones, after all. I believe he chose the right people for his team, you among them. You saw the miracles. You know they were real. What happened?"

He laughed. "That's not all! He told us that if we want to merit eternal life we will have to eat his body and drink his blood. Did you ever hear of anything like that! He said he was giving up his life for us and that we should do this in his memory. He said his death and resurrection would take away the sins of the world, and that his Father in heaven had sent him here to live on earth specifically to be this sacrificial lamb."

I remembered John had called Jesus the Lamb of God that day at the Jordan River. I couldn't understand the concept of eating his body and drinking his blood. It was a mystery to me. But if that's what it would take to merit eternal life then I believe it should be done. I wasn't going to make Peter's mistake of trying to rationally understand everything. If Jesus said that's what I needed to do then that was good enough for me. I couldn't explain it, but I believed it.

And if Jesus said his body was a temple and that he would be resurrected in three days I believed that too. A lot of things were falling into place for me.

But not for Judas. He was having none of it. For one brief moment I was sure I was looking in the face of the devil himself, so contorted were his features, so twisted and snarling. Suddenly, he got up. "I gotta go" he said.

"Where are you going?" I asked. I wanted to follow this guy, maybe even protect him from himself. And I wanted to warn Jesus.

"Gotta meet some people," was all he said. He got up to pay the innkeeper. As he did so I noticed his purse was very heavy, almost overflowing with silver coins.

There must have been at least thirty of them.

In the Garden

> And he came and found them sleeping, and he said to Peter: "Simon, are you asleep? Couldn't you keep vigil for even one hour?" Mark 14.37

I TRIED TO FOLLOW Judas as he left the inn but I couldn't keep up with him. He moved so fast; he was like a man possessed. He definitely wanted to get somewhere and do so in a hurry. Finally he stopped to take a breather and I caught up with him. I asked him again where he was heading in such a rush.

He was out of breath, but he managed to croak out the words, "I have to get back to the supper. Some of the men don't even know that I left, they were so mesmerized by the fantasy stories about resurrection and eating his body and drinking his blood. He looked at me and said I should go and do what I needed to do. And do it quickly." I thought this surely meant that Judas had to pick up some food or supplies for the meal.

I wasn't sure what kind of supper he was talking about, but I thought it probably was a typical Seder. But before I could ask him anything else he took off again, this time even faster than before. I tagged along as best I could, and, panting heavily, I was able to keep him in my sight. Soon he stopped in front of a rather large two-story house. He stood there, looking upward and shaking his head, as I finally caught up with him.

"I'm too late," he said, "They're gone." I asked where he thought they went. "Oh, there's this garden where he likes to go and pray.

I don't like the place, myself, and neither to any of the other guys. We usually just stay back in a clearing while Jesus goes further into the garden all by himself. We often take a nap while he's in there praying. Sometimes he has to come and wake us up. He's not happy when he has to do that."

I asked him if I could come with him to this garden. I was intrigued by its mysteriousness and possible danger.

"No!" His voice thundered. He glared at me with a look of pure contempt. "Get out of my way!" he shouted. "I know who you are, always poking around, pretending you're one of us, always trying to get his attention. It's almost like you want to be an apostle too!"

Then it was no longer Judas, but a hideous monster that stood before me: his face grotesquely contorted, elongated and engorged twice its normal size; his ears sprouted like pointed horns; his nostrils flared even wider than before and his teeth were chisel-sharp fangs. His eyes flashed red, and when he opened his mouth to speak, flames flared forth accompanied by cruel laughter and shrieks. A greasy drool ran down his chin and a putrid odor permeated the air. I could barely breathe.

My heart froze and I fell to the ground. Judas did not even look back as he began to run to the garden. I felt I had looked into the face of pure evil, and I had better get to that garden to warn Jesus. I got up and started running after Judas. He turned on me and my legs stopped working. I was petrified with fear and by the power of his gaze. I knew now I was not dealing with any normal being.

He took off running and I slowly got to my feet. I hobbled after him and ducked into the bushes whenever he turned back to look at me, his eyes flashing red beacons. His voice grated like stones rattling in an empty clay vessel. I shuddered when I heard him growl: "Jesus is doomed, don't you understand? He wanted to die and he will!"

I tried to move but I was like a man paralyzed, totally confused and helpless before this otherworldly power. He kept going, on his way to murder Jesus. But I could not let it happen. I struggled to my feet and staggered after Judas, who was now just a speck fading in the distance.

Finally I arrived at the garden. I couldn't see Jesus so I hid behind some thick shrubbery to see when he would appear so I could warn him. Peter was there, talking with the other apostles. He said Jesus had already come down once to wake them from sleep and he didn't want it to happen again. I think he knew something was up with Judas but felt confident that he could prevent anything that the traitor had in store. He bragged that he would stand up for Jesus and never deny him. Ever the faithful leader, he urged the others to also stand firm.

Before I knew it there was a horde of people converging on the place, soldiers with clubs and swords, and some Pharisees and priests as well, with Judas as their leader. As soon as Jesus heard the tumult he came into the clearing. He looked terribly agonized about something. He had to know what was going on. Judas went up and kissed him. Immediately the soldiers surrounded Jesus and put him in chains. He made no struggle, but, in a pathetic attempt at defense, Peter pulled out a sword and hacked off the ear of one of the soldiers. Jesus immediately restored it. The apostles took off running; and, I hate to say, so did I.

I heard later that they took Jesus to be tried by the Roman governor, a man named Pontius Pilate. I wanted to hear the proceedings but, because of the tremendous crowd, I couldn't get anywhere near the place. But as I slowly made my way home, exhausted and aching in mind and body, I could not fail to hear the cries that pierced the quiet of the night like a lance. Raucous shouts of "Crucify!" Then, "Barabbas!" And again: "Crucify Him! Crucify Him!"

I wondered if Jesus knew that I had tried to stop Judas from this murderous treachery. I tried to make a difference. I really did, but it was like me fighting against the devil himself.

It Was a Miserable Night in The City

Peter ran to the tomb and, stooping down, saw the burial clothes laying there and wondered what had happened.
Luke 24.12

JERUSALEM WAS A mess. The earthquake that followed the gruesome death of Jesus on the cross had leveled much of the town. There was debris everywhere. The city was enveloped in smoke from dozens of fires. The temple was in ruins, the sacred veil torn to shreds. Everyone was scared, even the Pharisees. There were reports of long-deceased spirits walking the earth, their graves ripped open by the violent tremors. The crying of children and frantic barking of dogs filled my ears.

As I wandered aimlessly through the deserted and burning city, I reflected on the events that had preceded this disaster: the triumphal entry of Jesus into the city; my bizarre confrontation with Judas and his satanic transformation right before my eyes; the agony in the garden and the ruthless arrest of Jesus; the horror of his phony trial; the duplicity of the crowds, the same people who had been singing hymns and strewing branches before him just a week ago now yelling "Crucify him!"; his painful crucifixion; the sight of Mary his mother beneath his cross; and finally his burial in a tomb donated by Nicodemus.

My hopes died with the thud of the stone as it was rolled into place to seal the tomb. The Roman soldiers stationed there looked confused as to why they were given the assignment to guard this corpse. Did Pilate really think the dead body would attempt to roll away the stone and break out of the bonds of death? Or were his friends going to steal him away in the middle of the night? That was laughable. That bunch of cowards was nowhere to be found, as they had disappeared when he was arrested and had not been seen since. Tough Roman soldiers, they were embarrassed to be given such a useless assignment. It would be an easy but boring night for them; they would probably fall asleep.

Certain events stood out in my mind as I recalled the past few days. Though I could not keep up with Judas, as he was moving under diabolical power, I later learned that he had recovered at least a semblance of decency and, overwhelmed by guilt, had returned to the temple. There, he threw the thirty pieces of blood money at the feet of the priests, acknowledging that he had given an innocent man a sentence of death. His body was later seen by many as it hung from a Redbud, a beautiful flowering tree that I fear will forever be tainted with the name "Judas Tree."

Almost as depressing in my memory was the sight of Peter, who had promised to forever stand beside Jesus, sheepishly denying that he even knew him. Not once, but three times, he had been asked by strangers if he was part of Jesus' group. Each and every time he failed to live up to his commitment to his leader. Three times he failed as a man and as a disciple, and revealed himself to be a coward and braggart. It was the most disgusting sight of my entire life and made me cry for how it must have hurt Jesus. He gave Peter a pathetic gaze when he heard him deny his name. Peter, his Rock. I don't think even the blows of the soldiers or the crown of thorns were as painful for Jesus as this most bitter betrayal.

And if Peter, the leader, the Rock, had failed so pathetically, what of the other disciples? I heard they were in hiding, fearful that the same crowds that came for Jesus were out looking for them. Their main concern, as usual, was for their own safety and welfare. Jesus had told them that they would be pursued and persecuted, just as he was; and that they would be hunted down and put to death. They didn't want to hear that and now they were scared out of their wits.

Almost as cowardly as Peter was the Roman overseer named Pilate. What a clown! Unable to man up and see that justice was done he caved to an insane mob. How can a person in authority even think, even less actually say, "I see no guilt in this man, therefore I will flog him and release him." Where is the logic in that statement? If the man is innocent, let him go free. If he is guilty of something, punish him. But it makes no sense to say, at one and the same time, that he's innocent and therefore I will punish him. For what?

But out of simple stupid fear, he gave in to the mob and released a convicted criminal instead of doing the right thing and letting Jesus go. Washing his hands, I presume he meant to absolve himself of his guilt. But I'm sure his cowardice will be remembered whenever people read the story of Jesus. I prayed that in the future our land would have better leaders with more fortitude and substance. But I fear Pilate, Caiaphas, the Pharisees, and all the rest of their ilk will always be with us.

The whole gloomy mess overwhelmed me with the sad realization of the apparent futility of the life and deeds of Jesus. I had been convinced that he was what he said he was. That he was the Son of God. All his wondrous deeds and miracles made that obvious to me. But now, despite all that, a doubt was beginning to grow in my mind. How could he have let this happen?

I heard that he spent a rough night in that garden just before Judas and his thugs showed up. He was heard crying out about a cup passing from him; but also, that he must drink it. I had no idea what was in that cup or why he was so frightened by it. If he was the Son of God couldn't he just say no?

He kept agonizing over that cup, and how his Father had placed it before him. I never met his Father but Jesus clearly had respect and love for him. He said that his Father had sent him here precisely so that he would suffer and die. But why? He was to take away our sins. But we must believe in him to be saved. We must drink his divine water that will never let us thirst again. He himself is to be our food, and it is by consuming his flesh and blood that we will obtain eternal life. I could not understand this, although I believed it. It remains a mystery to me, and I guess it always will.

In my despair over this miserable night and this miserable town, I had completely lost track of time and place. The situation was so depressing that I just didn't care; I didn't care if I ever ate or slept or even lived anymore. In my mind Jesus had held up a candle of hope for our poor wretched world and foolish mankind had forcibly snuffed it out.

As I found myself standing near that fateful Redbud tree, the thought passed my mind that perhaps Judas had the only answer that made sense on this miserable night.

It was late. Or rather, it was early. I had spent the entire night in my sad reverie, and now the sun was beginning to poke into the eastern sky. I didn't care. I had nothing to look forward to. My days, which had always been full of excitement and anticipation because of Jesus, now promised to be a sequence of endless boredom. I felt that a very real part of me had died with him.

I searched my memory for a saying or a deed or a promise of Jesus that would make sense for me. I prodded the very depths of my faith. I mused over the past years, over the many times I had heard him speak, sobbing as I recalled his commands and precepts and rules for living. All I had learned and seen and experienced with Jesus flashed across my mind.

I remembered his fixation with water, how he could even walk on it and calm it when it got stormy. How he produced a boatload of fish for Peter, and fed a crowd with bread and fish. I smiled through my tears at his love of children and the warmth and friendship he shared with Lazarus and his sisters.

My brain ached at the intensity of my effort to encompass the whole of Jesus. I remembered the crippled man at Sheepgate, and the homeowner whose roof was torn apart. I also thought of the Samaritan woman at the well, the woman taken in adultery, and the ten lepers he cured. I tasted again the fine wine he conjured up at Cana; and I remembered his tantrum in the temple, and what he did there. And what he said there. And then it hit me! It had been there all along, before my very eyes but I didn't see it. Now I did!

The temple! Of course, the temple! That was it! The temple was destroyed but it really wasn't. My mind was foggy as I tried to recall his exact words: "Destroy this temple and in three days I will rebuild it." We all thought he was talking about the temple building, but we were wrong! He was talking about his body. Judas told me that Jesus said his body was a temple. I didn't understand then but now it was crystal clear.

The rising sun marked the beginning of the third day! The temple was indeed destroyed, but the body of Jesus...his temple, was not! Overwhelmed with excitement, I just couldn't think any further. I realized that I was now sobbing uncontrollably.

Suddenly I heard shouts coming from the direction of the tomb: loud, exuberant, joyous shouts. My heart almost jumped out of my chest at what I saw next. The Apostle John was racing up the street. "The stone! The stone!" he cried. Then I saw Peter, coming after him. He was out of breath, but managed to pant, "It has been rolled away! The tomb is empty!"

Someone asked "What about the Roman soldiers, the guards?"

"They're gone," John said. Peter added, "the burial garments are still there, but the body of Jesus is gone!' He had recovered his voice now, confident that something miraculous had taken place.

He looked at John and they shared a knowing look that confirmed their faith that Jesus was alive. Then, I was amazed when they looked directly at me and nodded, as if they knew who I was! Everyone was shouting and congratulating the two apostles, who tried, but simply could not control their glee.

I overheard some of the murmurs, questions and comments that arose in the crowd surrounding John and Peter.

"Nobody could have moved that stone."

"It was too heavy"

"It's been three days."

"He said he would come back."

"Maybe he truly was the Son of God."

My eyes opened wide when I heard that. Is it possible that God so loved this world that he sent his son to suffer and die to save it? Is it possible that a man can be killed so brutally, be buried in an unassailable tomb, and still come back to life?

Of course it is, I thought, if that man is Jesus, the Christ, the Son of God.

The morning sun was beginning to blaze on the horizon. My mood brightened with it. Exhausted and hungry, I left the celebration and headed for home. On the way I passed the large house to which Judas had led me. Somehow, I felt drawn to it. He said they had eaten supper there, and it was there that Jesus had told them his body and blood were to be their food.

I went in. The house was vacant. Judas told me they had been in an upper room, so I went up the stairs and pushed the door open. The room was empty, the table bare except for a plate of bread and a water jug. I was surprised to see the jug looked exactly like mine. Unconsciously I moved to the table and sat down.

I was convinced someone had prepared this for me. Someone knew I would be coming here. Why else would I be so intently drawn to this house and to this very room? The bread was crisp and fresh. I poured some water to wash it down.

But it wasn't water that came out of the pitcher! It was wine! An excellent wine, a wine whose taste I remembered ever since that day at Cana.

I was suddenly aware of his presence. He was here! He had set this table for me. He had led me here to share this most precious gift of his own body and blood. I couldn't see him, but I didn't need to. I didn't know how or why this was happening, but I believed it was real and was overjoyed by it.

As I savored the wine and the memories it evoked, I was overwhelmed with love for Jesus. I felt one with him. He had taken over my life; now he had taken over my soul as well. I loved being so close to him. I wanted to be united with him for all time.

Awaking from my ecstasy, I went down the stairs and entered the bright, clear daylight squinting and smiling, my faith confirmed by an unexpected gift of bread and wine.

Saying Goodbye

> There are, however, so many other things that Jesus has done, which, if they were all described individually, the entire world could not contain all the books that would have to be written. John 21.25

IN THE PARTY atmosphere that prevailed on that bright morning, I actually had the opportunity to talk to the Apostle John for the first time. It was not the last.

In one of our discussions, he told me that he knew who I was, that all the apostles knew who I was, and that Jesus knew who I was. At first, they were concerned when they noticed that I was always hanging around and following them so eagerly. They were skeptical and thought I might be a spy for the Pharisees or some other enemy of Jesus. I was astounded to learn that there was even talk that I might be the one who would hand Jesus over to the authorities; that I was the betrayer!

I remembered that Judas said they all knew who I was, but I never thought that I might be compared with him! Eventually they came to realize that I was just an innocent, but very interested and harmless bystander. I told John about my Jesus diary and he said he was writing one also and that maybe we could compare notes someday.

He said that Jesus knew of my desire to be involved in his movement, but did not want me to be an apostle. Instead, he felt there were roles I could play in the future growth of his mission.

He told the apostles to keep an eye on me and to make sure I stayed loyal to his cause. There was no doubt of that!

I think I always knew in the back of my mind that Jesus would have to be aware of me and my interest in him. I was not invisible! But it was nevertheless heartening to hear it confirmed by one so close to Jesus as John, his favorite.

John also informed me of a few other things that not many people were aware of. He admitted it was not he and Peter who discovered the empty tomb, but Mary of Magdalen; and that Jesus had appeared to her, announcing his presence simply by calling her name. She then told John and Peter, who came and saw for themselves that the Lord was indeed risen.

He also told me that, shortly after the resurrection, Jesus appeared to them in the room where they were hiding. He walked right through the locked door, and greeted them with a single word: "Peace." They were amazed to see the Lord, alive and healthy, but still bearing the wounds of his terrible ordeal.

John added that Thomas had not been there when Jesus appeared, and, when the others told him about it, he doubted that it was really Jesus. I was not surprised at this because he always seemed skeptical, even from the first moment I saw him. He insisted he would have to prod the very wounds of Jesus before he would believe. He wanted to know.

Well, John continued, Jesus showed up another time when Thomas was there and gave him that opportunity. Then he told him: "Thomas, you believe because you have seen, but blessed are those who have not seen, yet do believe."

There it was again, I thought. That emphasis on faith as opposed to knowledge. If you don't believe something until you know it with your senses, what good is your faith? John pointed out that it was exactly that sort of logical thinking that caused Peter to almost drown.

Then John told me a surprising story. He said that, one day, he, Peter, and a few of the other apostles decided to go fishing to catch something for supper. They were at the shore of Lake Tiberius.

The fish were not biting, however, and the evening turned into night, and then night turned into morning, and still no fish appeared. Finally, they gave up and headed back to shore. By now, they were almost starving.

They were surprised to see a man standing on the beach, looking at them intently. He called: "Did you have any luck, boys?"

Peter called back, "I don't think there are any fish in this lake!"

They all laughed. They had heard that line before. John teased Peter with, "Do fish even exist?" Now the stranger joined in the laughter.

Then he said, "Cast your nets on the right hand side and see if you get anything." They rowed out a bit and tossed their nets as instructed. Immediately they were filled almost to breaking. In fact, the catch was too heavy for them even to get it into the boat.

John said he now became suspicious and wondered who the mysterious stranger might be. He whispered to Peter, "I think it is the Lord." Peter gazed at the figure on the shore, and said, "I think you're right," and immediately jumped into the water and started swimming to shore. The others followed in the boat, dragging the net full of fish.

When they got to the beach, there was already a charcoal fire going and a few fish cooking on it. The stranger said, "Bring some of your fish here so I can add them to the fire. Then we'll have breakfast."

"Our hearts were burning at this point," John said. "But no one dared to ask, 'Who are you?' So we sat down. Then we noticed that our host had a small loaf of bread in his hands. He broke the bread and gave it to us. We knew right then that it had to be Jesus!"

On another occasion, John told me about two apostles who were on the road to a town called Emmaus. He said they were met by a stranger who joined them on the road. He asked them, "Have you heard any news lately?"

They said, "Are you the only person in Jerusalem who doesn't know what took place there this past weekend?" He asked what had happened.

And then they told him that their leader had been arrested, tortured and put to death. But now, after three days, some of his followers discovered that his tomb is empty and no one knows where the body is. "Some say that he has risen from the dead, but nobody knows for sure," they said.

To their surprise, the stranger then explained to them the whole story of the savior as told by the ancient writings and the prophets. "Don't you see?" he said. "All this was foretold ages ago. He had to be betrayed and to suffer and die a horrible death, and be raised again."

John said they were so taken with the wisdom of this stranger that they asked him to stay with them for dinner. He agreed, and, while they were at table, he took bread, blessed it, and gave it to them.

"Their eyes were immediately opened," John said. "But, just as soon as they recognized Jesus, he vanished from their sight!

"It was the breaking of the bread that convinced them," he continued. "The same ritual he performed with us that evening when Judas betrayed him. We will never forget that night and what he said and did at the last supper we ate together."

John continued, "The two of them immediately turned back and returned to Jerusalem, they were so eager to tell the others about their experience on the way to Emmaus. But when they got there they were surprised to learn that everybody already knew that Jesus was risen and, in fact, had seen him too.

"Then," he added, "right there, while we were all together talking about him, Jesus suddenly appeared before us. 'Peace be to you,' he said. 'Don't be afraid.' We thought he was a ghost! But it was indeed Jesus."

John didn't tell me about any more appearances of Jesus, but I didn't need anything more to be convinced that he was risen from the dead. I believed it. I never doubted it. He said it would happen and I believed him.

After hearing these stories, I felt confident that John and Peter and the rest of the disciples were well-qualified to carry the story of Jesus throughout the Mediterranean area and maybe even to Rome.

Jesus told them he was going to a place where they could not go, but that they would see him again someday. I felt this meant that there was room in his Father's house for all who believed in him, and especially for those whose sins he had forgiven. He said he had come to call sinners to repentance by offering life-giving water and the precious gift of his own body and blood.

The apostles were on fire with a drive to spread the new faith everywhere they went. They couldn't stop talking about Jesus; no one ever could once they had seen him in action. I hope this same enthusiasm continues to motivate the followers of Jesus until the end of time, when he will come again as our judge, but especially as our savior.

I was sorry to see him go. It was over thirty years ago when I first set eyes on him as a little babe in Bethlehem. I was about twenty-five years old back then. Now, I am beginning to feel my age. We have gone through a lot together, Jesus and I, with me, often unnoticed, at his side.

My dreams of apostleship were never realized, but I think I may have helped his effort by keeping this diary. Someday, I hope, somebody will read it and become entranced with the story of Jesus, just as I was.

Given the political realities of this age, with Rome constantly rattling its sabers and weak leadership in my country, I'm not really sure what the future holds for me. But I do know one thing for sure: one day I will see my Jesus again. I hope he will recognize me. I hope he will know how much I love him.

I can't wait.

Acknowledgements and Thanks

I AM MOST GRATEFUL to my son, Jeff Mishur, for invaluable assistance on style and presentation. He is a master of the spoken and written word. Constant support and assistance have also been forthcoming from my dear friend Kaylee Kuenstler, who has provided as good a photo of this author as can be expected. Special thanks to Rev. Dr. Sharon Colbert Garretson for scriptural and doctrinal assistance. Louis Kehinde read the text and offered advice and suggestions. In addition I have benefitted from the support and encouragement of family and friends, including my new friends at Xulon Press. My sincere apologies if I have inadvertently forgotten anyone who rendered assistance in any way.

A Note on Sources

THE MAIN THRUST behind this book comes from an unexpected source. In *The True Believer*, longshoreman turned philosopher, Eric Hoffer, chronicles the typical "mass movement" from its birth as a radical concept propounded by one charismatic leader through its growth spurt and ultimate decline as it becomes an institution with a structure and full-time management. In doing so it loses the "passionate intensity," of which W.B. Yeats writes in his 1920 poem *The Second Coming*. Perhaps our world of today needs a recommitment to the passionate intensity the apostles and early Christians had for Christ and his message.

I must acknowledge, with humility and admiration, Archbishop Fulton Sheen's *Life of Christ*, and *The Passion and Death of Our Lord Jesus Christ*, by Archbishop Alban Goodier, S.J.; as well as a marvelous little book called *Tales from Holy Writ*, by Helen Waddell.

An interesting opinion on the role of Judas in salvation history is presented in a 1999 book by Professor Jerry Harvey, titled *How Come Every Time I Get Stabbed in the Back, My Fingerprints are on The Knife?* Other relevant background reading includes *The Truth about St. Joseph*, by Maurice Meschler, S.J.; *The End of the Modern World*, by Romano Guardini; and *The Old Law and the New Morality*, by P.J. Gannon, S.J.

The "Our Father" is rhapsodized beautifully in *The Vision of Prayer* by French poet Charles Peguy. The Gospel stories of Jesus and John the Baptist are corroborated in contemporary history in Book XVIII of *The Antiquities of the Jews*, by Flavius Josephus.

Chapters 13 and 14 of the Old Testament Book of Leviticus provide detailed information on laws and proscriptions concerning leprosy. For information on Greek and Roman deities and their role in Roman life I have relied on *SPQR*, by Mary Beard, as well as the *DK Illustrated Dictionary of Mythology.*

For the Gospel narrative I have consulted the traditional Confraternity Edition as well as the more contemporary translation from the original Greek by James A. Kleist, S.J.; The English Standard Version; The Living Bible, from Tyndale House; and the New Testament in Greek and Latin. Introductory verses preceding each chapter are my own translations from the Latin.